To Mark
My dear gen....
Love Pat xx

Dead Ringers

Trish Harland

ISBN: 148391206X
ISBN-13: 978-1483912066

DEDICATION

For Elaine
Without whose help and support this book would have remained an
impossible dream.

ACKNOWLEDGEMENTS

Special thanks to Elaine for reading the initial manuscript,
for invaluable assistance, advice and encouragement
during the writing of this book.

The life of every man is a diary in which he means to
write one story, and writes another.
~ James Matthew Barrie

God has given you one face, and you make
yourself another.
~ William Shakespeare

Prologue
October 30th 2009

A few thin ribbons of white cloud drifted aimlessly across an otherwise perfect blue sky. Rays of sun filtered through the autumn canopy of red and gold, casting light and shade on the russet carpet of the fallen leaves below. Dried and made brittle by the Indian summer, a grey squirrel rustled through them searching for 'winter larders' to horde its cache of acorns and wild hazelnuts. Alerted by the sound and movement the man stopped digging. His back straightened but his lower body remained hidden by the hole in which he stood. As he stood, perspiration gathered on his brow beneath his unruly mop of dark hair and dripped down into his eyes, momentarily blinding him. Irritated, he wiped them with the heel of his hand anxious to focus and locate the source of the sound. He looked towards the gap in the hedge and to the house beyond. As expected, nothing to see, nobody there because today he was home alone. They'd flown out of the country yesterday as they did every year at this time, albeit a week later than usual because rich bitch wanted to support some charity function at the Racecourse. Now and for the next six weeks he was master of all he surveyed, alone to put his well-rehearsed plan into practice. Ears pricked and eyes ever watchful he rotated slowly on the spot. His eyes finally rested on the small copse which separated the estate from open farmland. Then he spotted it, the squirrel,

0

motionless, clinging to the trunk of a nearby tree. Climbing out of the hole he closed in as quickly and quietly as the leaf covered ground would allow. The squirrel remained inert. He swung the shovel, sensing it the animal scampered out of reach a split second before the makeshift weapon smashed into the bark. Annoyed, his efforts thwarted he cursed out loud "bloody vermin" turned on heel and stomped back to the task in hand. Within minutes his mood had lifted as he stood and admired his handiwork. The shallow grave was ready, waiting to receive its deserving occupant. Not one he'd chosen but the one who, by her very presence, continued to blight what could have and should have been his perfect life. One to join the other resurrected women, now tenants residing in this cul-de-sac of death. Five sapling cypress trees marked the graves of women whose only crime was to remind him of a childhood best forgotten. Never again would they feel the warmth of the sun or admire the beauty of an autumn day.

Feeling good and stretching to relieve the ache in his muscles he smiled and said "tomorrow mother, I'll plant your tree tomorrow and then your final resting place is ready".

PART ONE

1

Flat 43a Salter St, Newbury, Berkshire
Monday November 2nd 2009

We Will Rock You' blasted out from the radio alarm clock
waking Laura with a start. She glanced over to the bedside
table; it was 6:45am on Monday morning, the start of what
was supposed to be a relaxing week off work. Shit, she
hadn't reset the alarm but, then remembering last night, she
hadn't expected to sleep. But she had and now it was over
six hours since she last checked the time. Angrily, she
reached over and cut Freddie off mid-lyric. Much as she
loved Queen, any sort of music was a no-no this morning.

She'd found herself alone in the king-size bed so Danny
boy hadn't crept back late and slipped in beside her. It
must be getting light outside, but the bedroom was pitch-
black. He'd insisted she swapped the flimsy curtains for
heavy drapes when he'd moved in, said he couldn't sleep
unless the room was in complete darkness. She'd willingly
agreed to change them although she'd always welcomed the
morning light streaming in through the large bay window.
But then compromise comes easy when you think you're in
love. This morning she wished she hadn't bothered, he was
totally inconsiderate and completely selfish. A phone call

4

would have been nice but obviously as far as he was concerned their relationship was far less important than nights out with his mates, drinking himself senseless.

Since Leo, his so called 'best friend', had returned from a year's stint in Saudi, Dan had spent more time with him than he had at home with her. She'd only met Leo once and hadn't liked what she'd_seen. An egocentric womaniser he'd flirted outrageously with her, in front of Dan, and she wasn't impressed. After Leo left she said as much but Dan had just laughed and said "That's just Leo, he's a great guy really". Dan had probably crashed at his flat last night, ok, so now he would be free to crash there permanently. Enough was enough; she wanted someone to share her life, someone who was mature and committed. What she had was a 32-year old jack-the-lad who was not long term partner material.

The decision made, she jumped out of bed pulled on her old jogging suit and, after a brief visit to the bathroom for a much needed pee, pulled down the light excluding drapes. The curtain pole on which they hung fell noisily to the floor. Another complaint from that cow, Josie Farnham, downstairs and the thought, despite her anger, brought a fleeting smile to her face. She left the drapes where they had fallen and turned her attention to Dan's clothes. Catching sight of herself in the mirrored wardrobe door she grimaced. Her normally attractive face was red and blotchy, her eyes looked like piss holes in the snow and it was definitely a bad hair day. Ugh, she thought, not a pretty sight. Opening the sliding doors she pulled his clothes off hangers and out of drawers, then crammed them unceremoniously into his old black Nike holdall. Again, a smile played on her lips as she screwed up all his 'designer' gear so that it would fit into the one and only bag he owned. She struggled to close the zip and in doing so managed to trap part of his favourite grey sweater. She didn't care, so what if it was ruined when he tried to unzip the bag. She was hurting and any grief she could cause him was just fine by her. Neatness was usually important to Laura and probably irritated Dan but today bollocks to it. She strode through to the kitchen tossed his bag down by the radiator and thought goodbye and good riddance Dan Williams.

Still infuriated and working on autopilot she prepared toast and freshly brewed coffee. The minute she sat down to eat the anger that had given rise to the frantic activity turned to despair and the tears began to flow. Danny should be here, they should have woken up together, made love, made plans for their week off, sharing all the things that make two people a couple. A knock on the door startled her. So he'd forgotten his key again had he? Hurriedly she took a handful of tissues from the box and wiped her eyes. You don't tell someone it's over through a torrent of tears. She stood up and walked to the door, opened it fully ready to launch into an angry tirade but it wasn't Dan. Instead a green suited Paramedic stood there.

2

Laura, surprised, just stared at the stranger. He was tall, around six feet with dark hair and incredibly blue eyes.

"Yes?" she said, finding her voice.

"You called for an ambulance Mam?"

Puzzled and still angry Laura replied vehemently.

"No, but my boyfriend might need one when he finally shows his face".

"But this is 43a Salter Street isn't it?" he grinned.

"Yes, so?" she sighed, already bored by the presence of this uninvited visitor.

"Whoa there Mam, I'm just following up on an emergency call that, supposedly, came from here 15-minutes ago. Apparently there'd been an accident and a man was seriously injured and needed our help".

"No one's injured yet, I'm the only one here and I certainly didn't phone for an ambulance."

"Not that I disbelieve you but can I just check inside?"

"Help yourself but you won't find anyone here, injured or otherwise."

Laura flounced down the hall and he followed closing the door behind him.

"I thought you guys came in pairs", she said.

"We do", he replied. "Roy's parking up outside. I came in

8

quickly. Our control room said the call was urgent."

She turned and as she was about to speak his fist slammed into her face.

The last thing that Laura heard as she slipped into unconsciousness was the sound of splintering bone.

3

1990

The boy was terrified; his heart was thumping, filling his head with noise. No room for anything but that one persistent sound. Time stood still, was it minutes or hours since he'd been thrust into this dank dark cellar. Long enough for him to reflect on his short life and wonder why the kind, gentle woman, his once beloved mother, had turned into the hard uncaring stranger that punished him for anything and everything. It was impossible for a nine year old boy to understand. He wished his dad was still here. Everything had been great when his dad was here. He'd been part of a normal happy family. It was almost a year to the day that his father had walked out of their lives. Monday June 4th 1989, the worst day of his young life, a day he wanted to wipe from his memory. He couldn't, it was ingrained there. The weekend had been so much fun. His dad had spent much more time than usual with him, playing cricket and football in their garden, even taking him to the local pub for a glass of lemonade and a packet of his favourite cheese and onion crisps. He remembered the pretended look of disapproval from his mother as they arrived home late for Sunday lunch. Then Monday arrived and, as usual, his dad left the house at 7:05am to drive the short distance to Didcot station where he caught the 7:30

train to Paddington. He'd always worked in London but liked to live and relax with his family here in the heart of Oxfordshire.

That morning was the last time he'd seen his father. The phone rang at 6:30pm. His mother had answered. He watched as the look of disbelief registered on her face and saw the floods of tears that followed when she realised that this was her husband's cowardly way of saying goodbye. He vividly remembered throwing his arms around her waist in an effort to comfort her repeating "what's the matter? What's the matter mummy?"

Why had his dad left them, where had he gone and would he ever come back? These were the unanswered questions that filled his head. He felt so lost and alone and thinking about his father only added to the boy's despair.

His mother, distressed as she'd been on that awful night, seemed to cope well with the fact that he'd gone. But as the weeks passed he began to notice changes, gradual at first. The house became untidy and uncared for. His mother, normally meticulous about her appearance, left her hair uncombed and her clothes unwashed.

And then the punishments started, just slaps at first but for the last few months she had been locking him in the cellar more and more frequently and for longer periods each time.

She knew how much he hated the dark. And now he was here again, this time his only crime was to ask for a drink. Arriving home from school hot and thirsty and finding his mother in the kitchen, in a seemingly good and friendly mood, he'd asked politely for a glass of water. She became enraged, taking him by the scruff of the neck and slapping him viciously until he'd started to cry and then pushing him into this dark and lonely cellar as she screamed "Constant demands that's all I get from you. I can't stand the sight or sound of you for another second". Remembering, he started to cry again.

His mother sat on the stairs, completely unaware of the boy's distress. Her grip on reality was fast disappearing and her descent into madness almost complete. She focused what was left of her mind on Harry, the errant husband. Would Harry come home tonight, surely he would come home tonight. Then a flash of reason told her he wouldn't be home tonight or any other night. The boy must have driven him out. Well he would pay. She would make sure of that.

She walked into the kitchen and started to prepare Harry's tea. The boy was still crying.

4

June 4th 1989

Harry hung up, Isabelle's disbelief still ringing in his ears. He felt sad that it had gone so wrong. They'd met when he was just 23, during the second year of his PhD at the London School of Hygiene and Tropical Medicine (LSHTM). He was a handsome young man with regular features, a dimpled chin, a mop of thick dark hair and deep set blue eyes, who'd always put study before pleasure in his bid to become Dr Harry Berriman. Not the medical doctor he'd once dreamt of becoming but a research scientist, an expert in immunity to tropical diseases. Since his involvement in a World Health Organisation project in Africa when he was in Sixth Form College, it had been his ambition to help rid the continent of diseases such as Malaria and Dengue fever. Not an ambition he was likely to fulfil single handed but at least he could play his part.

He wore heavy dark rimmed glasses not through necessity but in the hope that they made him look intelligent. Completely unnecessary, he was intelligent. He'd gone to the library to work on his thesis and there behind the help desk, long blonde hair, fine features and a beautiful smile, sat Isabelle. Stunning thought Harry, and he was smitten and all thoughts of study disappeared in an instant. She'd always seemed vulnerable, like a beautiful fragile butterfly, and it was these very qualities that first attracted him to her. After he qualified he was offered a junior research post by George Jensen, Professor of Immunology at LSHTM. With a job secured and his foot on the career ladder the first thing he did was to ask Isabelle to marry him. They rented a flat nearby and were ecstatically happy. Within a few months Isabelle became pregnant and Harry, though delighted, was concerned about the financial impact on their lives. Fortunately, shortly after their son was born Harry was promoted to junior lecturer which more than compensated for the loss of Isabelle's salary. A small baby and a small flat were not ideal so they decided to move out of London and find somewhere in the county that was an easy commute away. They had great fun searching for their country cottage and finally settled on one in Sutton Courtney, a pretty village situated on the banks of the Thames in rural Oxfordshire. The cottage was ideal for them, yes it needed work but it was habitable so they could move in straight away and do the work as and when the cash became available and, a big bonus, it was only minutes away from Didcot station and a direct rail link to London. In fact the perfect place to raise a family and live happily ever after or so Harry believed. But even the best laid plans fail, from the moment they moved Isabelle began to change, the traits that had once made her so attractive began to irritate him. She didn't make any friends and relied on him to be her sole companion. As their son grew it became just the three of them and he began to feel trapped and restricted by her possessive love. For the next seven years work was his only salvation, as soon as he boarded the train in the morning he felt free. His research was going well, he'd been promoted again and he enjoyed the company of his colleagues in the department.

Penny Glover, a 28-year old Oxford graduate, had joined the research team just over a year ago and, pushed together because of their work, they soon became firm friends. She was tall, around 5'10" only an inch or so shorter than him, dark hair, dark brown eyes, a friendly no-nonsense kind of girl. No great beauty but none-the-less attractive and, most importantly, his intellectual equal. Most people look forward to Fridays so they could have a weekend away from work but Harry began to loathe them. To him it meant two days away from Penny. He realised he needed a strong, independent, partner to share his life. They began an affair in May 1988 and the first time they made love Harry knew that what he'd felt for Isabelle was well and truly over. Isabelle was a passive partner never initiating sex. She always yielded without complaint allowing him to use her body sexually without actively participating. Penny on the other hand really enjoyed their passionate encounters. Last summer they'd taken a day off work, driven to the country and hired a rowing boat for the day. After half an hour of rowing Harry was sweating profusely and as they passed a water meadow covered in waist high grass Penny insisted he stop.

"Secure the boat and we'll take a stroll" she'd suggested.

About ten yards from the river bank she pulled him down into the uncut grass.

"Now make me sweat a little too", she said seductively, and there in the open air, with the long grass flattened beneath them they became locked together in a passionate tangle of yearning flesh. So when in February 1990 two 3-year research posts for a Senior Research Scientist and a Research Assistant working in the Immunology department studying Parasitic Diseases came up in equatorial Africa, Harry seized the opportunity for them both. His one regret was leaving his little boy but he had to leave Isabelle for his own sanity, he just hoped his son would someday find it in his heart to forgive him.

He turned towards Penny with a cheesy grin.

"Okay sexy", he said, "that's the hard part over. The rest of our lives start here".

She tucked her arm into his as they headed towards the

departure lounge at Heathrow.

5

November 2nd 2009

The man looked at Laura lying motionless on the floor and felt a momentary pang of regret as he realised her nose was probably broken. He took the photograph out of his pocket, she hadn't changed a bit. The same blonde hair, the same cute turned up nose, the same trim figure and, as always, she looked beautiful. The others had disguised themselves somewhat but not enough to fool him. Laura Marks hadn't bothered to hide behind another image. She'd simply changed her name.

Revenge may have been the motive for the first capture and killing and revenge had been sweet. Now revenge wasn't his only motive, now it was pleasure too. He enjoyed the search, the planning and the execution.

A delivery of post through the letterbox startled him and swiftly brought him back to reality. Now wasn't the time to get distracted. He had to move quickly before she regained consciousness. He removed the syringe from his pocket and injected the Ketamine into a vein in her left arm. That would keep her quiet.

Satisfied that she would be helpless for the next few hours

he stepped over her prostrate body and moved down the hallway. Finding the bedroom door ajar he pushed it open and went inside. Seeing the unmade bed, curtains on the floor and the drawers open and in disarray he thought 'untidy bitch deserves all she gets.' He smiled at the thought walked over to her dressing table and picked up a lipstick. 'Bright red, perfect,' he thought as he wrote MOMMIE DEAREST on the wall above the bed.

The police were no closer to tracking him down. It had been two and a half years now since he'd buried his first victim. Like most psychopaths he always followed the same pattern, almost as if it had been genetically programmed; day one abduction, then confinement and finally on day five, the best of all, internment. That gave DCI Burton and his bungling plods a fighting chance to find them, seven days in total, five above the ground and two below.

Mostly he liked to see the fear in the eyes of his mother as she realised she wasn't going to be rescued. Burying her alive was the icing on the cake. Fitting punishment indeed for the crimes she had committed against him.

No DCI Burton this time, he was history. Now he had a brand new adversary. He'd read about DCI Jake Summers and his appointment to replace the dead man. Knowing the enemy was important so he made sure he knew all there was to know about Jake Summers and his team of detectives. Watching them, following them and reading about them could be useful to a man who wanted to retain his freedom. Burton hadn't caught him and nor would Summers, 'but hey, game on Jake,' he thought. 'This is my 6th abduction, your first of course. You won't have a clue because I won't leave a clue. No contest, end of story.'

He picked up Laura's quiescent body and carried her out to the car. Even if they were seen who would suspect a paramedic and his patient? After all the medical profession was perceived as the good guys, there only to help and serve the public.

6

November 2nd 2009
20 Claremont Gardens, Newbury, Berkshire

Dan struggled into an upright position, peered through bleary eyes and tried to remember exactly where he was. As the room came into focus he saw other bodies littered around the floor and then he remembered, bloody Leo had talked him into staying over after their boys' night in. His head was thumping and his mouth felt thick and dry and suddenly a cup of black coffee seemed like a very good idea. He stood up and unsteadily picked his way through the prostrate bodies, stepping over Buzz, who was snoring loudly and almost blocking the kitchen doorway. In the kitchen he found Leo looking as fresh as a daisy dressed in navy chinos, white open necked shirt a navy cravat completed the ensemble, and he was already tucking in to buttered toast. His short dark hair was brushed, his blue eyes clear and sparkling. As always he looked immaculate.

"Okay Danny boy, good night eh?"
"God Leo, how do you do it, I feel like shit and you're scoffing toast".
"Practice my dear boy something you're sadly lacking since the delectable Laura moved you in".
"Not funny Leo, we did agree to live together. Why the

hell am I here when I should be at home with her?"
"Why indeed? Feeling guilty dear boy, well don't blame me
no one twisted your arm."

Dan was angry but Leo was right, he did feel guilty. He
hadn't even bothered to call her last night and, in fact, he
really hadn't given her a second thought. He poured
himself a large mug of black coffee and leaned against the
fridge marvelling at Leo's powers of recovery.

"I need to go", he said unconvincingly.
"Expecting a frosty welcome then?" Leo laughed,
"Probably but well deserved wouldn't you say? I'm 32 for
God's sake, it's pipe and slippers time in most men's lives
at this age. Why do I feel trapped? I love her but I can't
seem to commit in the way she wants."
"Then adopt my philosophy, mate, love 'em and keep 'em
on the back burner."
"Very cynical Leo but that's not me and you know it."

Leo was a string saver, he had this list and if he needed a
woman on his arm at an important function, one to
accompany him to the theatre or one simply for sex if he
felt horny, they were just a phone call away. They stayed
on his list hoping one day they might become the first Mrs
Leo Masterman.

"No chance," Dan said.
"What?"
"Nothing, just thinking out loud."
"Come on then, drink up and I'll give you a lift home."
"No thanks, I'll walk. I need fresh air to clear my head.
It's still fuzzy from the booze I poured down my throat last
night."

Half an hour later Dan opened the door to their flat.
"I'm home Laura", he shouted.
Then his world was turned upside down as he walked
through the flat and realised that something was very, very

wrong.

7

November 2nd 2009
Newbury Police Station Berkshire

DCI Jake Summers was feeling a real sense of foreboding and frustration as he contemplated the open files that littered the top of his desk. Frown furrows spoiled his otherwise handsome face. With his hands clasped firmly behind his head and leaning backwards against the wall on the precariously balanced chair he was deep in thought

It was November already and nothing had happened. In April 2007 the first victim had disappeared and every 6-months since another had joined her. Newly promoted, Jake had inherited the case from DCI Chris Burton. Five months ago his predecessor, 48-year old Burton, had suffered a massive heart attack and died instantly. Of course everyone said it was the stress of this inquiry. No bodies, no witnesses, no progress. He came into the job inheriting five missing women with no clue as to their whereabouts. Jake knew in his heart that they were almost certainly dead. Maybe one could be restrained for a long period but five, virtually impossible. Chris Burton was a good cop. He and his team left no stone unturned in their efforts to track down the women, but they had disappeared without trace leaving behind frantic families and friends, people who, understandably, were pushing for answers. Without bodies the only evidence linking the crimes was the victims' similarity in age and appearance and the fact that all the missing women were from the neighbouring counties of Berkshire and Oxfordshire. However, the most significant clue convincing him that the offender was one and the same were those bizarre words, the individualized 'calling card' left at the crime scenes. His modus operandi (MO) was obviously successfully allowing him to operate undiscovered and remain at large for so long.

Frustrated, Jake unclasped his hands and ran his fingers through his short black hair and sighed.

A knock on the door made him jump, almost upsetting his balance and dumping him flat on his back.
"Come in", he shouted, recovering quickly.
DS Maureen Connolly poked her head round the door.
"Mo", Jake said as he looked up, fixing his eyes on her as she entered the room. She avoided his stare and he knew immediately it was bad news.

"Looks like another one Guv. There's a guy downstairs, Dan Williams, says his girlfriend, a Laura Marks, is missing. He's noticed blood on the floor in the hallway of their flat and those dreaded words 'Mommie Dearest' are scrawled on the bedroom wall."
"And I was just thinking November's here already and no abduction, maybe it's over. Maybe he's stopped, maybe he's banged up, hopefully he's dead. Wishful thinking eh! How wrong can you be; the nightmare's not over, it begins again." Jake sighed.
"I was never convinced that the six month gap was part of the ritual Guv, probably more about opportunity."
"Okay Mo put Williams in Interview One, get the address and some keys and arrange to get crime scene officers to the flat pronto. Sounds like we have another abduction to investigate. I'll be there soon, just let him sweat for a few minutes."

Mo disappeared and Jake, gathering up the files from his desk, cursed in frustration.

In Interview Room One Mo switched on the tape recorder as Jake entered the room.
"DCI Jake Summers has entered the room, also present DS Connolly and PC Evans", she said.

Jake sat down next to Mo and across the table from Williams. Evans loitered by the door in case of trouble.
"Mr Williams. May I call you Dan?" asked Jake.
Dan nodded yes.
"I'm Detective Inspector Summers. My Sergeant here tells me you think your girlfriend is missing. So what makes you think that?"

Dan looked up into the blue almost violet eyes of the cop called Summers and thought 'those eyes are wasted on a bloke. He seems young to be a DCI, in fact doesn't look much older than me.' But Jake Summers was a good cop, and good cops are fast tracked in the force.

"Easy, Laura's disappeared, there's some blood on the floor in the flat and words I don't understand scrawled in lipstick above our bed. 'Mommie Dearest', what the hell does that mean? Laura's not a mother and she doesn't even like hers. It just doesn't make any sense. She's missing, I'm worried and I come here to report it and now I find myself in here being interviewed by a senior police officer and everything I say being recorded. You're freaking me out!"

Dan Williams seemed nervous and on edge. He was in his early thirties, unkempt and wearing a worried expression. He peered at Jake through bleary brown eyes that were clearly trying to focus. His tousled auburn hair curling round his ears and the nape of his neck was uncombed, he hadn't shaved and his clothes were rumpled to say the least. 'Looks like someone had a skin full last night and slept rough,' thought Jake.

"Relax Dan, just routine. Before we continue, and if you're worried, perhaps you would like to call your Solicitor, or would you like us to assign one from the duty roster?"

Dan looked scared and pale.
"I don't need a bloody solicitor. I haven't done anything," he said.
"Good. So tell me, when did you last see or speak to your girlfriend, Laura is it?"
"Sunday evening about 7pm in the flat. We had a bit of an argument about me going out again. She doesn't like my mate Leo much. I didn't intend to stay over at Leo's flat but I had a bit too much to drink. You know how it is Inspector."
"So the last time you saw Laura she was angry?" Jake asked.
"No not so much angry as disappointed that I was going out again," replied Dan.
"You go out quite often then and leave her alone in the flat?"
"Not really, a couple of times a week."
"And do you always stay out all night?"
Hearing the disapproving tone of Jake's voice Dan Williams had the decency to blush.
"No, of course not. Last night was the exception not the rule. I'm not some sort of alcoholic that gets plastered every night."
Jake, aware that Williams was embarrassed and getting angry, changed tack.
"Are you aware that we're looking for a serial abductor? The abduction cases, five in all, have been given massive coverage by the local and national press for over two years now."
"Oh God no, I have seen the reports but the possibility that she'd been taken by him never crossed my mind. Do you think she has?"
"Anything's possible, but I'm afraid we have to assume the worst. From the details you've given us his signature is

written all over it."

An hour later Jake was pretty convinced that Williams knew nothing about Laura's disappearance. He'd spent the evening, as he'd stated, drinking and playing cards at his friend's flat, finally collapsing on the sofa there. He hadn't arrived back at the apartment until 10am this morning. He was obviously upset and continually blamed himself for what had happened. His constant lament being "I shouldn't have stayed out all night."

Jake sighed, having heard it for what seemed the hundredth time.
"Okay Dan you can go, but don't plan any trips without informing us. We may need to talk to you again. Doubtless you'll be the centre of media attention so we'd be grateful if you don't discuss details of the case with them or anyone else. Any contact with the press should go through us; we don't need cranks or copycats hampering this investigation. And if you remember anything, however insignificant, let us know."
"Such as?" asked Dan, "I've told you everything I know."
"Did Laura mention any new acquaintances? Was she worried about anything? Did she mind being alone in the flat? Had she lost any keys? Anything at all really. It just seems odd that there's no sign of a break-in, not in this or any of the other cases."
"Okay, okay, point taken", said Dan. "I'll think about it. Anything to help, I just want her back, let me know the minute you have any leads."
"Oh by the way", Jake added as an afterthought, "do you have anywhere to stay, your flat is a crime scene at the moment, we don't want you in there contaminating any possible evidence?"
"I suppose I can ring my mate Leo", answered Dan.
"Okay just give my Sergeant an address where we can reach you, oh, and we'll need a recent photograph of Laura."
"There's one on my bedside table at the flat, taken about a month ago, you're welcome to take it", said Dan.

As he walked out of the office Dan took out his mobile and rang Leo.

"Hello mate, its Dan, can I crash at yours for a few days? Yes I know the Police have been onto you. No Laura hasn't thrown me out; I'll tell you all about it when I get there."

"I'll be at 20 Claremont Gardens", he said turning to Mo.

Mo raised an eyebrow.

"Your friend must be well-off to live there".

"He is. Don't forget to let me know if there are any developments, you've got my mobile number."

"You'll be the first", Mo said, "I'll see you out.".

8

Mo wandered back into Jake's office and came face to face with a very angry man.

"This arrogant bastard thinks we're all stupid and I'm beginning to think he's right. All we seem to do is wait for the next victim to disappear and hope he'll make a mistake. We don't make any headway in between."

Jake had made his reputation by solving difficult cases and had rapidly risen through the ranks because of it. But this case was different, pressure from the top, from the press and from the victims' families were taking their toll. He was beginning to think the unthinkable, that this case would beat him just like it had beaten the unfortunate Chris Burton. A stupid thought crossed his mind 'better get a medical'.

Mo, understanding his frustration, decided to take the positive approach.

"I need to get over to the crime scene Guv; I'll take DCs Gregg and Miller and ask Inspector Leyland if we can use a couple of Uniforms to do a door to door in the neighbourhood. We might get lucky, someone could have seen something."

"Good, go see Barry Leyland", advised Jake, "I'll just phone the ACC, she wants to be kept informed of any developments in this inquiry and then I'll tag along too. I need to be hands-on from the start of this one, get a feel for the scene while it's still relatively fresh. Let's hope Dan Williams hasn't tramped his size tens all over the flat and buggered it up. And Mo, make sure you call Inspector Leyland Sir."

"Ok Guv," she said pointedly.

So he'd heard about Leyland through the grapevine had he, thought Mo. Soon after Jake had arrived, Desk Sergeant Doug Underwood had told her that Leyland didn't like the overfamiliar 'Guv' that had been adopted by CID since a certain Met Officer had arrived and introduced it. Apparently PC Evans had called Leyland 'Guv' and he'd immediately called a meeting of all uniformed staff and told them that in future all his men would address senior officers as Sir because he found 'Guv' unacceptable and disrespectful. At the time the first thought that came into Mo's mind was 'dinosaur'. She wondered now, after his comment, if Jake thought the same.

9

Jake picked up the phone.

"Jane get me ACC Davis please," he said. A minute later his phone rang, it was Helen Davis.

"Jake you needed to speak to me."

"Yes Mam, we have another missing woman, a Laura Marks reported missing by her boyfriend, Dan Williams, this morning. He last saw her about 7:30pm on Sunday evening and he got back to the flat about 10am this morning, so she could have disappeared last night or earlier today. We interviewed the boyfriend, he was very distraught and I'm pretty sure he knows nothing about Laura's disappearance. His alibi was corroborated by a Leo Masterman, the owner of the flat where he spent the night so I'm not treating him as a suspect at this time", Jake reported.

"Ok, as always I trust your instincts Jake, anything else?"

"I'm just off to crime scene with DS Connolly", he said. "Forensics are there already dusting for prints, looking for clues".

He heard Davis sigh before she asked if he thought it was the same offender.

"Yes Mam, same MO as before, no visible break in, same message scrawled on the wall, no doubt same person."

"Ok Jake. Well you're in at the start of this one, do your

best; we're all under pressure to catch this bastard. Keep me in the loop."

"Will do, thank you Mam", he said as he put the phone down.

He'd always liked Helen Davis, they had history. He'd first worked with her when she was a super in the Met and he'd been a young, keen DS. They'd really gelled when they worked a case together in 2001, the murder of five prostitutes in and around China Town. Code named' Shanghai Susan' the investigation initially centred on the warring factions within the Chinese community, but unconvinced that these were reprisal killings Jake told Helen Davis as much. After several wasted weeks, no progress and another murder, Jake was allowed to pursue his 'serial killer' theory. Within days Sam Simmons, a homeless itinerant preacher claiming to be God's disciple was arrested and charged with the murders. He was found unfit to plead and sent to a maximum security psychiatric facility where he would probably spend the rest of his days.

Helen Davis had been impressed by Jake's insight and dogged determination to solve the case. They were colleagues for a couple of years before she'd taken the Assistant Chief Constable post at Thames Valley police. Since then, according to her, she had followed his career with interest, being impressed by his arrest record and rapid promotion to DI. When Chris Burton died, Jake was her first choice as his replacement so she was quick to offer him the DCI job at Newbury. He hadn't jumped at the opportunity. He loved the hectic social life that was London and there was never a dull moment at the Met either. He would probably make DCI there within two years and besides it wasn't easy to fill a dead man's shoes, particularly one who had left behind so much unfinished business. The offer stayed on the table for a week before he contacted Helen and agreed to apply for the job, although he knew full well it was fait accompli if he wanted it. The breakup with Andrea had forced his hand and now he was wondering if maybe he'd made an error of judgement. The 'Top Brass' would certainly be scrutinising his performance on this case. It could make or, more likely break, him.

10

Jake left his office, ran downstairs and slid into the passenger seat beside Mo who was looking slightly impatient.

"Sorry it took longer than I thought", he said apologetically.

"No worries", she shrugged. "I thought maybe you'd changed your mind about coming. Everything ok upstairs?"

"As ok as it can be with five abducted women. No I think we can make that six missing and pressure from everyone mounting."

"Gotcha, let's get going then", she said. "Perhaps this is the case where we get lucky and catch the weirdo who's taking them. Inspector Leyland was happy to give us some Uniform backup for the necessary donkey work and I've got Dave and Dusty along to help where needed."

Jake turned and nodded to the two young detectives in the back. Dave Gregg was a wiry 25-year-old with sandy hair, twinkling blue eyes and a cheeky grin. Not conventionally handsome but he had what Mo called a nice face. He was a Londoner who had the annoying habit of peppering his speech with cockney rhyming slang. He was a plodder, happy to take instruction, thorough and reliable. Jake always thought he looked more like a barrow boy than a cop.

Alan Miller, Dusty to his friends, was a different kettle of fish. He had short dark hair, dark brown intelligent eyes, an olive complexion, undeniably British but often mistaken for a Latino. As he told everyone he got his good looks from his Italian born Grandfather. He was a graduate of Bath University, perceptive, intuitive, definitely one to watch and, of course, with those good looks the ladies loved him.

11

Salter Street

Five minutes after leaving the station Mo drew up outside the flats in Salter Street. Three identical buildings side by side, each building containing seven flats, three two-bedroomed on the ground floor and four one-bedroomed on the second floor. A small road at the side of the third building gave access to resident parking at the rear of the properties. Either side of the flats fairly new terraced town houses stretched the length of the street, only identifiable one from another by the colour of the front door and the brass number attached to it. The only access to the rear of the properties was through the house itself. Reminding Jake how much he disliked the concept of modern housing, phenomenal prices, no character and not very inspiring. If asked to describe them he would say aesthetically unpleasing and then he thought 'you snob Summers' and smiled. Directly opposite the flats, on the other side of the road, two large iron gates opened onto a small car park giving access to a large, mainly grassed tree lined area where people walked their dogs. To the left of the car park a small gate gave access through to a children's playground with swings and slides. Mini-golf and tennis courts were also facilities that would probably attract the locals.

Mo watched Jake appraise the area.

"You're looking at Linborough Park Guv", she said. "It's well used by the public and right opposite the crime scene. Maybe yield a witness or two, eh!" She sounded optimistic and his spirits rose.

"Hopefully Mo", he replied. "Ok uniform have just arrived, Gregg get them knocking on doors and talking to anyone that might be, or has been, in the park this morning. Anything out of the ordinary, any suspicious characters seen hanging around, vehicles not usually parked here, anything at all that is not the norm; tell them to get it written down. There's no such word as insignificant. Understand?"

"Earwig Guv", said Gregg. Jake's eyes rolled in his head. That must be rhyming slang for twig or understand.

"Good, ok Miller you come with us and we'll take a look see at this flat."

"It's on the second floor in the first block Guv", said Mo.

Each block was accessed through one main entrance where a brass plaque listed the numbers inside, in this case ground floor 41- 41b, second floor 42,42a, 43 and 43a. The front door opened onto a large square hall, in the centre a rather grand polished wooden staircase led to the upstairs flats.

"No lift then", Jake complained, as he took the stairs two at a time. The other two followed at pace.

Upstairs the door of 43a was open and criss-crossed with crime scene tape. They pulled on the obligatory white forensic suits, overshoes and gloves that had been left outside the door, ducked under the tape and entered the flat, which was a hive of activity. Jake spotted Inspector Mike Long, a square jawed no-nonsense Yorkshire-man, and the Senior Scene of Crime Officer.

"Found anything Mike? asked Jake.

"Small spattering of blood on the hall floor doesn't look like a major wound. It could be a nosebleed or something similar. Only her clothes in the wardrobe, his all seem to be crammed into that Nike bag in the kitchen. Looks as if one angry woman packed it or rather shoved the clothes in. Is the boyfriend a suspect?" asked Long.

"No chance, alibi checks out and he appears to be genuinely upset."

"Didn't think so, not unless he was responsible for the others too", said Long.

"So you think the same guy is responsible?" asked Jake.

"Pretty much, the circumstantial evidence points that way, so, sure as one can be without DNA. We'll take a break now, give you some space. We've lifted prints, taken a scrape of the blood which is probably hers. We're almost done here, just a few things to finish off when you've had a look see."

"Great, thanks Mike."

"Ok Mo, you take the bedroom", Jake said as they left. "Dusty get the living room and I'll concentrate on the kitchen."

"Got the photo of the vic", Mo shouted from the bedroom. "It's a good one, just head and shoulders. She's a good looking woman, same type as the others blonde, shoulder length hair, good bone structure, slim, yeah definitely easy on the eye".

"Ok bag it and we'll take it back to the station", said Jake.

Ten minutes later the three of them congregated in the kitchen.

"So, anything of interest?" Jake asked hopefully.

Mo answered first.

"DI Long was right, only female clothes in the wardrobe and drawers. Maybe she was about to dump Williams. There's a set of heavy window drapes lying on the floor, the bed's unmade and it looks like she slept alone last night, only one side looks dishevelled. Wardrobe door and drawers left open, otherwise the room's immaculate. Her clothes are neatly hung or folded, her shoes together in pairs on a shoe rack. The dressing table is uncluttered, definitely a neat freak."

"Nothing in the living room Guv, but like DS Connolly said she is one neat lady, not even a magazine lying around. Looks as if everything has a place and everything is in its place."

"Not so tidy in the kitchen, tissues dropped on the floor near the breakfast bar, toast and half a mug of coffee on the bar, the Nike bag flung in the corner by the rad."

"Any conclusions?" asked Jake.

"He interrupted her breakfast so she was almost certainly abducted this morning", Miller answered confidently.

"Good, anything else?"

"Normally keeps a tidy home, tissues on the floor, his clothes screwed up in that holdall, drapes down in the bedroom, he didn't make it home last night, I would say this was one pissed off upset lady. The other thing Guv, how did he know she was home alone, the abductor must have been watching and waiting for an opportunity", said Mo.

"Exactly Mo, ok food for thought. I think we're done here let's get back to the station and let forensics back in to wrap it up."

As they left the flat Jake signalled to Mike Long, who was standing by the side of his van devouring a beef burger.

"You'll never get any thinner stuffing yourself with that junk", Jake said.

"Well it is lunchtime and I couldn't resist when I saw him turn into the Park", Mike said, patting his distended belly and pointing to the burger van in the car park opposite.

"We've finished in there now", Jake laughed, "and we've removed her photo from the bedside table. Have you checked her car out back?"

"Yeah", Mike said. "Jonesie did that while we were inside, nothing obvious there, but we'll tow it and do a more thorough check at the depot. You'll get my report ASAP but you know how careful this guy is, he won't leave any clues. The blood will be hers and the fingerprints we've lifted probably all belong to the occupants of the flat, family or friends."

As they were driving back to the station, Jake turned to Dusty.

"Dusty, ring Dan Williams, see if he has any explanation re the drapes and his clothes."

12

20 Claremont Gardens

When Dan arrived back at Leo's apartment most of the bodies had dispersed, only Buzz remained. He'd moved to the couch and was still snoring.

As Leo opened the door the witty remark he was about to offer died on his lips. Dan looked awful, pale and drawn, shoulders slumped.

"Come in mate, what's happened?"
"They think the abductor's taken Laura. Oh God Leo it's all my fault, if I'd gone home last night she'd still be there."
"How did he get into the apartment?" asked Leo.
"I've no idea and neither do the police, definitely no sign of a break in. She either knows him or feels she can trust him otherwise there's no way she would've opened the door."
"But mate if you had been there and it was her he wanted you could have ended up dead in your bed."
"Better that than feeling I'm a real shit and have let her down big time."
"Bit extreme mate. They'll find her."
"Will they though? They haven't found the other five that disappeared."
"Who's disappeared?" asked Buzz groggily from the couch.

"No one, just a book I was reading" Leo interjected.
"You'd better get off now Buzz I've things I need to do."
"Not bed and breakfast then?"
Leo raised his eyebrows as he looked at the overweight, unfit Henry Buzzard.
"No sorry mate, need to get on."
Buzz turned to Dan "you coming too?"
Dan looked helplessly at Leo.
"No I want to pick Dan's brain about a computer problem I'm having. I'll be in touch", he said, pushing Buzz towards the door.
"Ok, ok, I get the message at least let me put my shoes on."

He left the apartment muttering about being tired and hungry.
"Thanks Leo, I don't want to tell the world and his wife how bad I'm feeling. If Buzz knows it won't be long before the whole of Berkshire does too."
"Not known for his discretion our Henry", Leo laughed.

The phone rang and he picked up.
"Yes he's here", Dan heard him say.
"A DC Miller for you mate", Leo whispered.
Leo listened as Dan talked.
"I don't know …. maybe, …. yes, …… it's possible."

"That was a very one sided conversation", Leo said two minutes later.
"I know but they were asking me things I can't answer. Someone had pulled down the blinds in the bedroom, taken my clothes out of the wardrobe and stuffed them into a holdall. They found them by the radiator in the kitchen. I think the most likely explanation is Laura was about to bin me. I didn't realise just how much I care about her till now. I'll make sure she knows when they do find her."
"Course you will mate", Leo said reassuringly, but secretly thinking 'if' they find her.

13

Newbury Police Station

"Dusty, try and locate Dave Gregg. If he's back here then both of you join us in the Incident Room."

"On my way", he answered, already halfway down the corridor.

Jake opened the door and walked into the Incident Room, Mo close behind.

Five photographs were already on the whiteboard, arrows and comments in red linking them together. Jake picked up the phone.

"Hi Jane, could you come to the Incident Room, pick up a photo and get it copied. Yes about six will do for now. Bring one back in and we can add it to the others on the board. Thanks."

Less than a minute later Jane picked up the photo.

"Ok, time to re-examine the facts", Jake said to Mo. "Before you say not again remember we have a new victim, a new crime scene and hopefully this time he's made a mistake."

"You know I'd never say that", Mo replied. "I'll go over the facts a hundred times if necessary. So now we have six missing women, my gut instinct tells me the first five are probably dead. I'm certainly hoping, as I'm sure you are that we can find this one before she suffers the same fate.

He always pens Mommie Dearest behind the bed at the scene", she continued. "Looking this up on the web we found quote ' *Mommie Dearest, best- selling memoir, turned motion picture, depicts the abusive and traumatic adoptive upbringing of Christina Crawford at the hands of her mother the screen queen Joan.*' I have read and re-read the book Guv and the daughter paints a very grim picture of life with Joan. From this, we're assuming, rightly or wrongly, that the abductor was abused by his mother or a close female relation. Because the victims are so similar in age, looks, etc., we have also assumed that the abductees bear some resemblance to the abuser and that she was probably in her mid-thirties when the abuse occurred. Was there a man involved in the abuse? Probably not; his victims have all been women as far as we know. Is the offender the child of a single or divorced parent? Is the abuser still alive, in fact is he still the victim of abuse?

Where does he take the victims? It could be somewhere fairly remote. From the moment of abduction they are never seen or heard of again. Why a 6-month gap between abductions? Does he work abroad? Is he only in the country then? Does he only have access to his holding place then? All his victims come from an area of about 30 square kilometres so is he local to the Newbury area or was it here that he was abused? How did he gain access to abduct the victims? We think he was granted access because there's no sign of break in at any of the properties. So we concluded that they either know him or they trust him. Who would women trust, a Vicar, a Policeman? Surely not a Politician." Mo giggled.

Jake picked up a book and slammed it onto the desk.
"Not funny Connolly, we've reviewed this case so many times and we pose question after question we have no bloody answers. It's all conjecture, no hard facts and you're cracking jokes. It's not helping, we need a break. Knocking on doors hasn't achieved anything so far."

"Maybe it has at last Guv", said Gregg, as he and Miller entered the room. "PC Martin, one of the uniformed officers, spoke to a woman who lives in the third block of flats. Fifty-three –year-old Sally James actually had some information for us. She works as a cleaner at the Dalton Abbey Primary School which is only a ten minute walk away from the flats."

"So? Get to the point" Jake said impatiently.

"She was on her way to work this morning about 7:30am and noticed a dark estate car parked in the layby near the flats. The only reason she noticed the car was as she passed it she looked into it and was surprised that all she could see was her own reflection. It was impossible to see if the car was occupied."

"I've heard about this film Guv", said Mo, "converts glass into a one-way mirror, you can see out but no-one can see in. The Library was so fed up with people walking into the glass doors there they had them covered with it as a safety measure. Why would anyone put in on their car?"

"They wouldn't unless they were up to no good. Did she get the registration?" asked Jake.

"No Guv just thought the car looked fairly old."

"Brilliant! Right get back to Uniform and ask them to check if any of the residents own a dark estate car with mirrored windows."

"Already done".

"Good thinking Gregg, Mo and Miller will bring you up to date".

14

Two hours later Mo reappeared in his office.

"Uniform hasn't found anyone claiming ownership of the said vehicle Guv. I've got copies of Laura's photo ready to hand out at the Press Conference. Reporters are crammed into the press room waiting impatiently for you statement".

"Ok I'm coming, wish me luck".

As soon as Jake walked into the room he was bombarded with questions.

"Quiet please", Mo shouted. "DCI Summers is not here to answer questions but to tell you the facts as we know them at this time. Please let's have some cooperation".

The room quietened and all eyes turned to Jake who began to read the statement he'd prepared:

At 11:15am this morning Laura Marks, 32, of Flat 43a Salter Street was reported missing by her fiancé, a Mr Daniel Williams of the same address. He returned to their flat after spending a night with friends. He expected to find his girlfriend there, instead the place was empty. He became alarmed when he noticed a small amount of blood on the floor in the hallway. There was no sign of a break in or a struggle. In fact Mr Williams thought that Laura Marks had just gone shopping until he saw the blood. Going through the flat he noticed other things that made him suspicious so he came to the Police

Station and reported her missing. After interviewing him for over an hour, and checking his alibi, we are satisfied that he is not involved in her disappearance. Because of the similarities between this case and other on-going investigations, we have reason to believe that the same person is responsible for this and the other five abductions that have taken place in the area over the last 30-months. Forensic officers have been busy at the scene and we have uniformed officers knocking on doors in the area looking for witnesses. Sergeant Connolly will distribute photographs of Laura and there are copies of my statement on the desk here in front of me. We need public involvement to catch this guy so please just get the information out there. Thank you for your attention.

If Jake thought it would be that simple he was sadly mistaken as questions were fired in from every angle.

"That's all I'm prepared to say at the moment. You will be informed as soon as we know anything but for now please just leave quietly and let us get on with the job."

Jake left the room with unanswered questions ringing in his ears.

At 6.00pm Mo knocked on his door.

"I'm off now Guv", she said, "see you in the morning. You should go too it's getting late."

"Already too late for some", Jake shrugged.

"I don't suppose you want to relax and enjoy a meal and drink with the girls?" Mo said on a whim as she could see his frustration.

"Why not, anyone ever tell you you're a life-saver Mo?" Jake grinned, his good humour returning.

When he called her Mo she knew she was back in favour.

"I'll just ring Jess; let her know there'll be one more for dinner."

He followed Mo to the car park and watched as she jumped into her almond green 1969 Mini Cooper S. Restored from a wreck, she'd bought for a pittance on-line, to a magnificent classic car courtesy of her father Ed who ran an auto body repair and renovation workshop in Stafford. Ed Connolly had come to England from Dublin as a young man, settled in the Midlands where he'd met and married Mo's mother, Jacqui. He worked for garage owner David Dennison, learned his trade and started his own repair shop in the eighties. After building a successful business he branched out into renovating classic sports cars, particularly the MG range. He still worked full-time but now his two sons were involved in the business as well.

Jake was envious, he loved old cars but with his six-foot two frame was only too happy to climb into his roomy BMW. Maybe one day he'd buy an old MGB and get Ed and the boys to work their magic on it.

Smiling, he followed Mo out of the car park. Normally socialising with lower ranks outside of work was a no, no, but Mo had been a real friend to him since he'd arrived in Newbury and he knew she would never show any disrespect or take advantage of their friendship. He began to relax looking forward to the evening ahead.

15

Sutton Courtney, 1990

The door of the cellar was flung open, the sudden influx of light made the boy cover his eyes and cry out with fear.

"It's alright, don't be afraid" a warm friendly voice called into the cellar. "You're safe now."

He blinked through his tears and looked up into the kindly face of a middle-aged woman who reminded him of his beloved and much missed grandma who had died when he was just six-years-old. The woman spoke again in a soft friendly voice. "Your mother has been taken ill and we're here to make sure that you're looked after until she's well again."

As Janet said the words she knew in reality that this little lad would probably be in care for the foreseeable future. She held out her hand and the boy got up and took it. "How did you know I was here", he asked, "did my dad send you?"

The woman looked surprised.

"No, your teacher Mrs Evans said you'd been absent from school for more than a week and she was very worried about you. We haven't seen your dad but now we know you have a dad we will do our best to find him, until we do we can provide a warm and pleasant place to stay."

"Will there be other children for me to play with?" he asked gingerly.
"So many, you'll wish for peace and quiet sometimes."
"No, I'll never get tired of hearing voices, I've been so lonely for so long", the boy said, as he smiled at Janet.

Janet's heart went out to the boy. Life was so unfair, all children deserved to grow up in the safe arms of a loving family. All too often she'd seen the psychological damage caused by abuse and cruelty. She hoped that this boy would be able to put the trauma behind him and, with love and understanding, become a well-adjusted member of the society that, up to now, had so obviously failed him.

Forty minutes later they were standing in the hallway of Stirling House being greeted by a couple in their late thirties. Janet introduced them as Rob and Jenny and explained to the boy that they would be his house parents and that, during his stay there, he, like the other boys, would be part of their extended family.

"I'll show you your room and then you can meet all our other boys", Jenny said as she stepped forward.
He clung fiercely to Janet's hand and she looked down into a face filled with apprehension.
"Don't be afraid Harry," she said stroking his head. "Go with Jenny, she'll look after you. Remember, you're in safe hands now."

Reluctantly he released her hand and taking Jenny's left the room.
They walked up a flight of stairs and along a narrow corridor stopping outside a room, the white door of which had a painting of a Robin in the centre and was named appropriately Robins Nest.

"We name all our rooms", Rob explained. "The next one is Sleepy Hollow", he said, pointing to another door further along the corridor. "You'll be sharing Robins Nest with young Johnny Price."

"Johnny, this is your new roommate Harry Berriman", Rob said as he opened the door.

A skinny, dark haired, dark eyed boy about Harry's age and size got up from his bed. "This is my bed you can have the one over there", he said. "How long are you here for?"

"Until my dad comes for me I suppose."

"A long time then, never mind, I've been here forever you'll get used to it. So you're Harry?"

"Yes Harry, Harry Berriman."

"Hello Harry" he said shaking Harry's hand. "I'm Johnny. You can be my new best friend."

And for the first time in a very long time Harry felt happy and safe.

16

Croft Cottage, November 2009

Mo Connolly pulled up outside her cottage in Hermitage. It was almost derelict when she and her partner Jess had bought it two years ago but it was work in progress and was gradually being restored to its former Victorian glory. Jess heard them arrive and stood in the doorway smiling and, as always, Mo thanked the Lord for her beautiful soul mate. At five feet five she was a couple of inches shorter than Mo but just as stunning. Large, wide set, dark brown eyes fringed with long dark lashes, long dark hair framing her oval face and a full lipped mouth added to her attractive appearance. Jake envied them; they were a happy loving couple at ease with who they were. He remembered the first time he'd met Mo, she was casually dressed wearing an oversized England rugby shirt tight black jeans tucked into a pair of grey Ugg boots and she introduced herself.

"DS Maureen Connolly Sir, no cracks please my gran was an ardent tennis fan so everyone just calls me Mo."

Jake, having no idea what she was talking about, just smiled.

"Hi Mo, DCI Jake Summers or Guv to you."

"No-one told you it was dress down day then Guv?" Her mischievous eyes appraising the tall suited figure before her.

"And there I was thinking you always dressed like a fly half."

She laughed, exposing white even teeth and he thought 'good looking woman with a sense of humour, we should hit it off'. A natural blonde, she was 5' 7" tall, slim build, short spiky hair, green eyes framed by long blonde lashes and a bone structure that most women would die for. He had been more than a little upset to learn that she had a female partner and was off limits. 'Well she would have been off limits anyway. Hanky-panky between ranks was unacceptable in Police circles' he thought. Now she and Jess were like the sisters he never had and he loved them as such.

Jake kissed Jess on the cheek as they went into the house.
"Good of you to take pity on this friendless soul", he said.

"Don't sound so pathetic Jake, you, friendless, never in a million years. You're just feeling sorry for yourself. Come through into the sitting room and meet my sister Jaime, she's staying here for a few weeks recovering from a broken heart and a broken leg. She had a riding accident which accounts for the broken leg and her horse Manhattan had to be destroyed hence the broken heart. I'll leave you two to chat and, who knows, you might cheer each other up. You, my love", she said turning to Mo "can help me in the kitchen."

Jaime was sitting by the glowing Inglenook fireplace and, if anything, was even more attractive than her sister. Dark brown eyes looked up at him. Her face was framed by wild dark red curls and, for the first time since Andrea, he felt a serious flicker of interest.

"Hi, Sorry I can't get up and shake hands but I'm incapacitated", she explained, pointing to her plastered leg.
"I've heard a lot about you from those two but I'm sure

none of its true."

"You have me at a disadvantage; I didn't even know Jess had a sister. Mo's never mentioned you." Jake smiled.

"Well Mo wouldn't, she thinks I disapprove of their relationship, which of course is hogwash. If Mo makes Jess happy then I'm happy. So you're the boy wonder who solves all the crime in West Berkshire."

"Hardly a boy", Jake laughed, "and definitely not a wonder but I do try and keep the locals safe in their beds, although at the moment we're having a tough time convincing them of that. But don't let's talk about work, it will only bore you and frustrate me."

Jaime smiled and thought good looking, good body, shame about the job.

"Drinks anyone, Jaime?" Mo asked as popped her head round the door.

"Glass of red please", replied Jaime.

"Jake?"

"Better be good I'm driving so I'll have a tonic please."

Mo disappeared and Jake turned back to Jaime.

"So what do you do when you're not busy breaking legs?" he asked.

"You make me sound like a gangster", Jaime laughed. Jake laughed too.

Mo came in carrying their drinks.

"You two seem to be hitting it off. It's good to hear you laughing again Jake."

"I'm just finding this so relaxing and a pleasant escape from police work" he said. "I was just asking Jaime how she earned a crust."

"You mean you haven't heard of Jaime Mason, famous crime novelist. She always gets her man!"

"Mo exaggerates", laughed Jaime. "I've only had a few short stories and a couple of novels published. Hardly famous."

"Perhaps she can help solve our case."

Jake shot Mo a warning look.

"Not a good idea to discuss any cases we're working on", he said.

"I wasn't serious, just making conversation. Relax Jake and enjoy the evening", she replied.

The tension was broken as Jess came in and announced that supper was served. As the evening wore on, although out-numbered three to one by women, he really began to unwind and enjoy himself. He found Jaime a delight, easy on the eye, easy to talk to and when they were left alone while the other two were busy washing dishes he bit the bullet and asked if he could see her again.

"You mean like go out on a date? she asked.

"Something like that", he replied.

"Sorry I don't date policeman I only write about them."

"Is that a no then?" he sounded disappointed.

"'Fraid so, my motto is never mix business with pleasure."

"We're hardly in the same business; you write fiction and I deal with real life villains but if that's how you feel forget I asked".

And then he was gone and she could hear him thanking and saying goodnight to Jess and Mo.

He'd sounded hurt; perhaps she'd been a little hasty in her decision. Too late, she doubted he'd ask again.

17

Donnington Village, Berkshire

Jake drove the four and a half miles home thinking about the evening he'd just spent with Mo, Jess and the lovely Jaime. Before he knew it he was passing The Carpenters Arms in Donnington, his local watering hole, saw Julie Meadows carrying in the menu board and waved. She either recognised him or the car, waved back and mouthed hello. A few moments later he pulled into the parking bay beside his ground floor apartment. Hobbs was sitting cross legged outside his front door looking inscrutable. As he approached the large marmalade cat got up, stretched and started to verbally chastise him for being late home. The cat had adopted him from the moment he'd moved in and when Chris Finch, his owner, had been posted from RAF Welford to another base miles away, Jake had inherited the demanding Hobbs. He opened the front door and Hobbs ran in quickly almost tripping Jake up.
"Dammit Hobbs, you've got your own entrance in the kitchen you don't need to wait up and give me grief."

Hobbs wasn't listening. He'd run through into the kitchen and when Jake got there was busy tucking in to the biscuits that had been left for him.
"I know, just like me, you don't like eating alone".

Jake went to the fridge took out a bottle of Pinot Grigio and poured himself a large glass. Hobbs looked at him disapprovingly.

"This is my first tonight", he said and took a large swig from the glass. 'God,' he thought, 'I'm standing here explaining myself to a cat. It really is time I sought some human company', which immediately brought Jaime to mind. He walked through into the sitting room, slumped down on the leather settee and turned on the TV. He watched the news which was all bad so he switched off and played some Kenny Gee music instead. Moments later Hobbs jumped up did his usual three turns and then made himself comfortable on Jake's lap. Jake felt himself relax as he listened to the haunting sound of the saxophone, making him appreciate the music and his surroundings. He loved this apartment the first time he'd seen it and now to see it filled with his things he loved it even more. He hated clutter and kept the furnishings modern and minimalistic. The front door opened onto a spacious hallway, the main bedroom with en-suite shower room was immediately to the left. It was a large airy space, containing a king size bed and bedside table. In an alcove next to the bed was a small dressing table and stool. Two sets of drawers, full length and short hanging rails and a shoe rack were hidden behind smoked glass, space-slide doors that filled the whole of the wall opposite the bed. The furniture was white, the carpet silver grey, the bed linen white with black and grey accessories and, to complete the décor, a black and silver striped Roman blind hung at the window, a man's bedroom. Next to the main bedroom a smaller second bedroom was used as Jake's office. A red futon was pushed against the wall and could be used as a spare bed if anyone stayed over, which his mother had been threatening to do since he moved in.

The main bathroom was to the right of the entrance and the rest of the apartment was taken up by the sitting room and the kitchen/breakfast room. The sitting room door led

out to a patio and small terraced garden. Yes he was happy
here, Andrea could've been happy here too, it was much
nicer than the pokey flat they'd shared in London.

He'd met the delightful doctor Andrea Lancaster at a
charity auction at St Barts in 2006. She specialised in
gynaecological cancer and breast surgery and was at the
auction hoping to raise awareness of breast cancer and to
raise money to support research into the disease. He found
it difficult to concentrate on what she was saying. She had
to be the most attractive woman in the room. She wore
her long dark hair in a chignon at the nape of her elegant
neck. Her curled dark lashes gave depth to her hazel eyes.
She was 5ft 11inches of pure woman and all Jake could
think of was how good those long shapely legs would feel
wrapped around his waist. They'd spent the evening each
absorbed by the other and Jake, reluctant to say goodnight,
thought a beautiful intelligent woman, I could spend my
life with her. After that first meeting he pursued her
relentlessly and within three months they were shacked up
together sharing a love of life, a love of frequent energetic
sex and a deepening love for each other. But they were
both very ambitious and furthering their careers meant
spending hours, that should have been together, apart and
the relationship suffered big time. It was a day or so after
he'd been offered the Newbury job that she told him she'd
fallen in love with consultant Cardiologist, Geoff Duncan.
End of happily ever after dream but tonight for the first
time he felt ready to move on with his life. Perhaps if he
persisted he'd be able to persuade Jaime to visit.

Hobbs purred contentedly.
The phone rang disturbing Hobbs and making Jake curse
out loud.
"Who the hell is ringing here at this hour?" Hobbs sprang
from his lap and Jake answered the persistent ringing.

It was his mother, who else.
"Jake I've been trying to reach you all evening. Where have

you been?"

"Out", he snapped. "I'm a big boy now Mother, I have a life, I have friends and I've been out to dinner with some of them tonight, okay?"

"I don't like you when you're snappy darling", she said in a hurt voice.

He relented.

"Sorry Mum bad day at work, what can I do for you?" he asked trying to sound pleasant.

"I phoned to tell you that Rory's back from Germany and the family will be staying here for about ten days. It would be nice if you could spend time with us too."

Rory was Jake's older brother by two years. A Major in the Military Police he had spent the last three years with the British Forces in Germany. He was married to the opinionated Glenda who could easily have run the British Army single handed and was always moaning that her Rory should at least be a Lt. Colonel by now. They had two boys, James aged eight and Guy who was almost six. Jake loved his brother and the kids were great, but Glenda, a couple of hours was the most he could manage in her company.

"That's great Mum, I'd love to see them but I'm up to my eyes in this abduction case so the most I could do is, probably, a Sunday lunch."

"Do try darling they would love to see you. So these friends you had dinner with, were they female?"

"Mother, mind your own business", he laughed.

"But Jake it is my business. Your brother had a wife and two children by the time he was your age. I'm just thinking we need more children in the family to perpetuate our good genetic lineage."

He laughed again; his mother had always been a bit of a snob.

"I'm putting the phone down now Mother, busy day tomorrow. I'll phone you about Sunday. Goodnight and

God bless", and before she could answer he'd hung up.

18

Chapelgate, November 3rd 2009

Laura gradually regained consciousness. She felt disorientated, she was aching all over, her head was pounding and her mouth was very dry just like having a bad hangover. And her nose, God her nose really hurt. She touched it gingerly, it felt painful and swollen and she could feel dried blood around her nostrils. As her senses returned she began to remember why. That bloody paramedic had hit her and obviously drugged her in some way. She looked around and found she was lying on a double mattress on the floor of what appeared to be a basement room or cellar. The only light came from a small table lamp on the cellar steps. Laura tried to sit up and found that she was manacled by her right leg to a chain that went round a concrete pillar about 6-feet away. As her eyes became more accustomed to the gloom she saw an unopened bottle of spring water on a small table to her right. Assuming it had been left there for her she shuffled on her bottom until she reached it then quickly unscrewed the cap and took a long swig from the bottle. As she drank she began to take in more of her surroundings. The room was large, probably about 30-feet square and smelled damp, although it wasn't cold. She saw the glow from what appeared to be a wood burning stove that was situated at the front of the space and beside it, against the wall, a wooden log store that was more than half full of neatly chopped logs. A rough-hewn work bench occupied the space near the cellar steps and tools of every kind hung above it. Weapons was her first thought. She stood up slowly and moved unsteadily towards it. She made it to the next support pillar then ran out of chain, still more than 10-feet from her destination.

"Shit, Bugger, Hell", she cursed, realising that her movements were restricted to roughly a 16-foot diameter circle, the centre of which was the pillar to which she was tethered. Disheartened she made her way back to the mattress. En route and within reach she came across a chemical toilet complete with a box of soft toilet tissue on the floor beside it and a small stainless steel sink with soap and towels. Fully equipped prison she thought as she sat down. Opposite the steps she noticed a black cloth that was draped over something hanging on the wall. What was covered up and why? Knowing it was futile to try to reach and uncover it she closed her eyes and said a silent prayer.

As she struggled to make sense of the situation the cellar door opened and her attacker switched on an overhead light and came down the steps toward her carrying a tray containing what looked like breakfast. The uniform had been replaced by jeans and a light coloured sweater and something about his face looked different, but Laura just couldn't bring it to mind. Probably because her fear was mixed with outrage at being held here against her will.

"What the hell is going on, why am I here?" Laura shouted, wincing with the pain and sounding much braver than she felt.
"You don't recognize me all grown up do you Mommie Dearest. You're at home again, at home with your son", he said, setting the tray down beside her.

If she'd been scared before Laura was really terrified now,

he wasn't making any sense and that made him very dangerous.

"I'm not your Mother. How can I be, I'm only 32 and you must be about the same age."

The man looked at her as if she was crazy. He pulled a photograph from his back pocket and thrust it into her face.

"Photographic proof, Mommie Dearest. You, me and dad before he ran off and left us remember?"

Laura focused on the photograph and sure enough she looked very like the woman in it.

"But if this was a photo of me I'd be over 50 now."

"That's exactly what you said last time", the man said, grinning "but I know who you are and you know why you're here. I've buried you five times already and then like a bad penny you turn up yet again."

"By the way", he said as an afterthought, and in a much nicer tone, "I'm afraid I broke your nose. Unfortunate but the bone's not displaced so the treatment's easy. I've brought you a bucket of ice so wrap some ice in a towel and apply it to your nose at intervals throughout the day, that will reduce the swelling. I've also brought you some painkillers and nasal decongestants so you'll be absolutely fine in a couple of days."

"I'll be fine will I, locked in this dungeon with only a madman for company. I need medical treatment, a doctor not a jailer."

"I'm a qualified Paramedic Mommie Dearest and you're the crazy one not me. Oh and don't waste your time screaming and shouting, no one can hear you."

"I already sussed that otherwise you would have gagged me as well. So where exactly are we?"

"Nice try but that's for me to know not you", he said.

"If you won't tell me that perhaps you can tell me what's hidden underneath that cloth on the wall?"

"Just some of my souvenirs. All will be revealed in due course. In the meantime enjoy your breakfast."

With that he left her alone again.

19

Newbury Police Station, November 3rd

Jake arrived at work early and as he walked through to his office he felt a sense of purpose in his stride, perhaps this would be a good day. Before he had chance to take off his coat Mo came running in.

"I think we may have another break Guv. A guy called Rob Bishop has just phoned in and, it's really uncanny, he said he's seen the woman before more than twenty years ago and she hasn't changed a bit. Weird or what?"
"Weird. So where is this strange man?"
"Stirling House. It's located in East Trenton and used to be a boys' home. The Bishops were house parents there until the home closed several years ago. The place is owned by the Local Authority and now it's used as a scout camp and Kindergarten. Apparently they still live there and act as resident caretakers and wardens", Mo replied.
"Get your coat Mo; we're paying Mr Rob Bishop a visit."

Thirty minutes later they were ringing the bell at Stirling House. The large Edwardian red brick building sat resplendent on about an acre of land situated down a quiet country lane on the outskirts of the town. The tarmacked area at the front of the house was marked out by white lines into parking bays. The rear was just laid to grass and the property was enclosed by a five foot high privet hedge. Beside the arched-topped panelled oak front door a brass plaque gave a potted history of the founder and benefactor, Sir Edward Stirling. Apparently he had commissioned the house to be built in 1910 to provide a home for 'boys in need'.

A tall man with a well-trimmed beard, thick grey wavy hair and twinkling blue eyes, in his mid-sixties, answered the door.

"Yes?"

"DCI Jake Summers and DS Connolly, we had a call from a Rob Bishop."

"Aye that'll be me then. You'd best come in."

He was dressed in a rough brown Harris Tweed sports jacket, dark green corduroy trousers, a green and brown checked shirt open at the neck and he spoke with a soft, almost lilting, Scottish accent.

They followed him into the spacious entrance hall. The walls were lined with wood panelling, behind the impressive staircase to the left of the front door was an unmanned reception area enclosed by a circular desk. A large colourful notice on a door just in front and to the left of the reception desk announced the presence of KinderKlass Kindergarten, pre-school education for 3-5 year-olds. The polished red quarry floor tiles conjured up a childhood memory of his grandmother kneeling down applying cardinal polish to her front step. Jake smiled at the thought.

"Incredibly quiet here for having a Kindergarten on site", Jake remarked.

"Half term", Rob said in explanation.

He ushered them into a large comfortable sitting room with a welcoming open fire.

Mo felt as if she was stepping back in time and into an Edwardian drawing room. The room contained leather buttoned furniture, a large sideboard and two small occasional tables. A bookcase filled the whole of one wall, a reading table standing close by and a grandfather clock ticked noisily in the corner. A red patterned carpet covered the floor. The fireplace had a fender, fire irons, including a poker, shovel and tongs for picking up hot coals, and a coal box.

Above the fireplace was an ornamental mantelpiece cluttered with ornaments and brass candlesticks. An over-mantel ornate mirror completed the illusion.

"Lovely room", said Mo conversationally.
"Yes it is, but not ours unfortunately. It's used solely for entertaining visitors. We have quarters upstairs", Rob replied. "Take a seat," he said, pointing to the brown leather winged arm chairs on either side of the fireplace.
"I'll get my wife Jenny to come down and join us. It was her that saw the news broadcast and actually recognised the woman."

Mo looked hopefully at Jake and feeling buoyant he winked at her. Moments later Rob was back followed by his wife Jenny, a small dumpy woman with a kind face and a welcoming smile, every inch the mother hen. Seeing the two of them together made Mo think of a modern day Queen Victoria and her Gillie, John Brown.
"Can I offer you coffee or some tea? It's no trouble, we like to make visitors welcome", said Jenny Bishop.
"Thank you, no," Jake smiled, "we're anxious to hear about the photograph and how you know the woman in it."
"I don't", said Jenny, and Jake felt his heart sink.
"But I do know a lad who carried her photograph everywhere with him for almost a year. Then it disappeared; he must have lost it although he was adamant that it had been taken."

"What lad?" Jake almost shouted at her.

"It was a young boy called Harry Berriman. He arrived here in 1990 and stayed with us until his sixteenth birthday. A bright boy, always keen to please, he befriended that awful Johnny Price for a while. Remember Rob?" she asked, looking at her husband for confirmation.

"Thick as thieves the two of them were for a while, never could understand why, different as chalk and cheese. Then they had a big falling out. Kids eh!"

Mo could see impatience written all over Jake's face.

"So Mrs Bishop the photograph, who was she?"

"Why, his mother of course. I could never fathom it, for over a year she'd physically abused him and he still wanted to be close to her, albeit through a photograph. You wouldn't believe the upset it caused when he lost that photograph."

"Can you remember why he was sent to Stirling House? Didn't he have relatives who could have taken him in?" asked Jake.

A flash of annoyance sparked in her pale blue eyes as she looked pointedly at Jake.

"I remember everything about all my boys, it was my job. Mrs Evans, his year five primary school teacher missed him in class and reported it to Social Services. They dispatched Janet Purvis to investigate. Nice woman, died last year. Anyway she found the mother in a wretched state, the house was filthy, Mrs Berriman was filthy, she'd gone completely doolally tap," Jenny said, tapping her forefinger against her temple.

'Mad then', thought Mo, never having heard the expression doolally tap. Jake was exasperated and thought, 'stick to the point woman or we'll be here all day'.

"Apparently the father ran off with another woman and in her confused mind she held the boy responsible. Of course he wasn't but nonetheless she subjected him to vicious beatings on a regular basis and often locked him in the cellar, or worse in the coal box in the cellar. Sometimes he was left there for days on end with only rats for company. In fact, I think he'd been bitten by them several times as he slept."

Mo winced, the poor little sod, left alone with a crazy woman and no one to look out for him.

"Did anyone try to trace the Father?" she asked.

"I think Social Services did try. He was supposedly in Africa, but by the time they found that out he'd moved on and the trail petered out, or so they said. More likely they couldn't be bothered to waste any more resources looking. Anyway, I do realise that this can't be a photograph of Harry's mother, she never regained her sanity and hung herself several years ago but honestly this missing girl is her double. Did she have a daughter that no one knew about?"

"No Mrs Bishop", Jake said, shaking his head, "it's just a coincidence. Can I ask you to look at these photos as well?"

Jake passed her the photographs of the other missing women and waited.

"Well I'll be damned", she said, "they all bear a striking resemblance to each other and to Harry's mum, although the one called Laura is most like her. I've seen these photos in the press as well but the likeness wasn't good enough for me to make the connection to his mum. These women, they're all still missing, aren't they?" Janet Bishop looked horrified.

Rob Bishop, who'd sat quietly listening to his wife, suddenly broke his silence.

"You think Harry has something to do with their disappearance don't you? You think he's wreaking revenge on his mother with these look-alikes."

"Don't be daft Rob", Janet scowled at her husband "our little Harry wouldn't do that. He wouldn't, would he Inspector?"

"We don't know anything at this time Mrs Bishop," Jake said, not wanting to alarm the couple further, "we are just following every lead and covering every possibility. Have you seen or heard from Harry recently?"

"Not recently. We had a letter about eight years ago from Australia didn't we Rob?"

Rob nodded his agreement.

"Harry immigrated to Melbourne. He wanted to set up his own business there. He was a qualified plumber, did his apprenticeship with George Jacobs one of the best in the business. He took Harry on after he left school, even had him lodging with his family. Yes, George took a real shine to the boy, wanted him to go into partnership after he qualified, which he did for a year or so. Then he had this hankering to go to Australia. Although the Australian immigration authority puts strict controls on the number of people entering the country each year they welcomed Harry with open arms. Here was a qualified plumber who could train and employ local people. We don't know how successful he was because we haven't heard anything since. So there, he isn't even in this country so he can't be responsible for these dreadful crimes."

Jake glanced at Mo with a 'there goes our suspect' look.

"Do you still have the letter Mrs Bishop?" he asked.

"I most certainly do, I'll run upstairs and get it for you", said Jenny as she hurried away.

"She thinks all her boys are angels Inspector", Rob said, "he was always a quiet lad, never any trouble, not like his pal Johnny but sometimes the quiet ones are the worst, if you know what I mean."

Before Jake could reply Jenny returned clutching an envelope which she handed to him.

"There, just as I said, still in the envelope with the Australian stamp on it."

"You've both been extremely helpful. May we borrow the letter for a while? We'll take great care of it."

'You'd better; I treasure the things that my boys send me," replied Jenny.

"Right Sergeant" said Jake, "we'd better get back to the

station. Once again thanks for your help, we may need to talk to you again, if we do we'll be in touch. I will personally see to it that your letter is returned."

Jake stood up, shook hands with the Bishops and headed for the door. Mo followed, re-iterating their thanks.

As soon as they were in the car Mo punched the air.

"Yes!!" she said, "finally, a bona fide lead, something concrete to get our teeth into."

"Don't get too excited, this guy is supposedly in Australia, or at least he was eight years ago."

"Guv, that's what is exciting, he could be anywhere now, a lot can happen in eight years. It certainly doesn't exclude him from the frame."

"No you're right, we have a lot of checking to do or I should say you have a lot of checking to do."

"Not a problem Guv."

"Organize a briefing for two o'clock, we need to liaise with Uniform and see if they have turned up anything else from the door to door, oh and see if you can get any leads on Berriman senior. I suggest you give that task to DC Jackson, our resident computer nerd, I'm sure he'll track him down even if Social Services couldn't."

"In which order?" Mo said laughing.

"You must learn to prioritize Connolly or you'll never make DI", Jake grinned.

Mo hadn't seen Jake this animated in weeks, purpose had returned and when Jake had purpose he was a force to be reckoned with.

As Mo drove back to Newbury she glanced at Jake's solemn face.

"You and Jaime seemed to hit it off last night", she said.

"Yes it was very refreshing to spend an evening with an attractive woman and not talk about work."

"May I remind you that you spent the evening with not one but three attractive women."

"You don't count Connolly you're spoken for, and she's available."

"I don't think Jaime would approve of the expression available Jake. She's a clinical psychology graduate, did a Masters with Gus Harrison, the criminal profiler, and then much to his annoyance gave it all up and became a successful author. She hasn't been in a serious relationship since dumping her last serial cheat about eighteen months ago. She has lots of friends, and that and writing seems to be enough for her at the moment", Mo told him.

"That, I believe. I actually asked her out last night but she turned me down flat."

"Oh, I think she's interested, she just doesn't know it yet. After you left it was Jake said this Jake did that."

"Don't you dare bull-shit me Connolly", he replied.

"Me Guvnor, never" Mo said, laughing.

"Something else to make you laugh, Hobbs gave me a bollocking for being late home", he said as he turned to look at her.

And she did laugh.

"I love that cat, so much character."

"You have him then."

"He chose you and you know full well that you'd never part with him."

"Yeah you're probably right."

20

Chapelgate, 2005

"Well darling what do you think of our new home? Perfect isn't it?" said Harry, swinging Penny around their large farmhouse kitchen.

"Absolutely", Penny answered kissing his cheek, "It couldn't be more perfect. Miles from anywhere, no immediate neighbours and now we can enjoy the lifestyle that we've worked so hard for, living in your beloved England and spending time in what's now our Portuguese holiday home."

After a year in Africa they were both totally frustrated. Constant battles against corrupt officials who pocketed money that had been allocated for their research projects had turned Harry the visionary into a very disappointed man. Deciding enough was enough they decamped and went to Lagos in Portugal to help Penny's Uncle George run his leisure craft company. Harry had an immediate rapport with the old 'sea-dog' and he became like a son to him. With George's help he learned all there was to know about boats and Penny was happy dealing with the administrative side of the business. Even in low season they were kept busy, so the company grew fast and flourished. So much so that they bought a café bar on the

Marina and named it Harry's Haven. With its picturesque view over the Marina and the good, home-cooked food it served, the place became popular with tourists and locals alike.

By the time George died in 2004 the businesses were worth several million pounds and Penny, being the only kin he cared about, was the sole beneficiary. They decided then and there to sell up, retire and live the quiet country life in rural England supplemented by holidays in the warm sun of Lagos, where they had lots of friends and a good social life.

Harry had found what looked to be the perfect property on-line and had travelled to England to look it over while Penny stayed in Portugal to sort out their finances. The first time Harry saw Chapelgate Farm he knew it would be their new home. It was no longer a working farm, the previous owner had sold off most of the land but the property had still been left with approximately four acres of land, several outbuildings and a small woodland area on its southern border. Chapelgate was located in the lovely Berkshire Downs, about a mile and a half from the nearest village and about three-quarters of a mile from the nearest neighbours. Newbury was only a 20-minute drive away so it was in the perfect position, with a village shop and a pub just down the road and a good sized town nearby. The house was only just visible from the road and was reached via a narrow un-adopted road which led to the large wrought iron gates that allowed access to the property.

Through the gates a sweeping gravel driveway led to the front of this imposing building. The outside of the property was impressive, covered in ivy and standing in an acre of formal gardens it looked like a smaller version of the main house in 'To the Manor Born' and funnily the estate agent showing him round was a ringer for Audrey Forbes-Hamilton. The inside had been sympathetically restored and was a pleasant blend of old and new that really worked.

"Well Mr Berriman" said the Audrey clone, "what do you think of it?"

"Quite magnificent" Harry enthused, "I'm sure my wife will love it too. I'll phone her tonight and get back to you tomorrow. Okay?"

"Oh good, yes that will be fine." Audrey, delighted, almost rubbed her hands with glee.

"The house is perfect", he told Penny on the phone that night, "the current owners have renovated to a very high spec, all we have to do is move in. The paint job may not be quite to our taste but that can be changed as and when. We have four acres of land, almost one acre of which has been landscaped into a series of interconnecting lawns, flowering bushes and trees and we even have a large fish pond."

"Whoa", she said, hearing the excitement in his voice, "sounds as if you've bought it already, remind me, how much does it cost?"

"£800,000 but I think there's some room for negotiation."

"A bargain then! Okay darling if you love it that much I will too. So do the deed, go ahead and buy it."

"Are you sure? Don't you want to see it first? I'll be spending a lot of your money after all."

"No need to see it, our tastes are very similar, I trust your judgement and anyway it's our money not mine. Don't forget you helped George build up the business that I inherited."

"I love you Penny Berriman."

"I love you too."

The next day he put in an offer of £775,000 on the property which was accepted. Now here they were six months later fully installed in their dream home, Chapelgate.

21

Incident Room, Newbury Police Station

Jake walked into the noise filled room at exactly 2pm. Uniform occupied most of the seats and a few CID detectives lounged against the furniture. Mo was sitting at the front desk trying to maintain order but everyone was talking at once and she wasn't hearing anyone or being heard.

"Quiet please" shouted Jake, "you'll all get a turn."
All eyes turned towards him and the room fell silent. He made his way to the front of the room and sat down beside Mo.
"I guess DS Connolly has brought you all up to date with the details we've gleaned so far?"
A low murmur of agreement filled the room.
"Good, ok, Barry you've been coordinating the door to door any progress?"

Inspector Barry Leyland, old school by the book copper with thinning brown hair, a military moustache and a ruddy complexion, stepped forward clicked his heels.
"Sir", he said, "we've done a house to house in Salter Street and in the adjoining Cranford Road. We haven't spoken to all the residents yet, some were out but hopefully we'll

catch up with them later."

"Fine, keep at it, this guy seems invisible, five abductions no witnesses. Surprise me, do we have any this time?"

"Nobody seen bundling bodies into cars, Sir, but PC Halliday spoke to an Alec James in Cranford Road who had been walking his dog on Salter Green about 7-o'clock yesterday morning. Halliday tell DI Summers what he said."

"I don't know how important this is Sir", Halliday said, standing up.

"Well we won't know 'til we hear it, will we Halliday?" Jake snapped, "Just spit it out lad".

The young PC's face turned scarlet, clashing with his almost orange hair.

"Sorry Sir", he took out his notebook and began to read from it.

"I spoke to a Mr Alec James of 24 Cranford Road at 09.35 this morning and as Inspector Leyland said he was walking his dog on Salter Green on the 2nd November at approximately 7am."

"Where the hell is Salter Green?" Jake interrupted.

"Locals call Limborough Park that Guv," Mo answered quickly.

"Right so we have one area with two names. I'm glad we cleared that up," he said sarcastically.

"Ok Halliday, what next?"

Mo shot him a sidelong glance that said 'give the boy a break.'

"Asked if he'd seen anything suspicious Mr James answered no. Asked if he had seen anyone in the vicinity he said yes someone dressed in what looked like a green uniform entering the first block of flats. Mr James said that he didn't think anything of it just, assumed that the guy lived there."

"So a witness saw someone going into the flats early on the morning in question and you don't think that's important?" Jake snarled.

"What does a green uniform suggest to you Halliday,

maybe a Paramedic or maybe an Ambulance driver? Barry, when we've finished here can you get some men back to Salter Street and check if any of the residents work in the Ambulance Service. Did he give you a more detailed description of the man Halliday?"

"White male, darkish hair, probably about six feet tall, too far away to see anything more than that Sir."

"Right, Jacko any progress on Berriman senior?"

"Work in progress Guv, he went off to Gabon with a woman called Penny Glover in 1989. They'd taken up research posts at the World Health Organization field station there. They left before their contracts finished and from there travelled to Lagos in Portugal where they were involved in the leisure industry, hiring out boats taking holiday makers out to see the Dolphin pods and running a café on the Marina. Seems the business flourished, in fact they amassed quite a fortune. The owner George Glover was her uncle and she copped for the lot when the old guy snuffed it about five years ago. The business no longer exists. It was sold to a Portuguese entrepreneur who split the assets into several companies and sold them on."

"So what happened to Berriman?" asked Jake.

"Not entirely sure yet Guv, but he's probably enjoying his retirement on the proceeds. There are several Lagos ex-pat websites that I can search."

"Good work Jacko, keep me informed. Ok, Sergeant Connolly your turn. Give us a resumé of the facts as we know them at this time."

Mo stood up in front of the whiteboard.

"Right Guv, we now have six missing women. Jennifer Rawlings aged 34 from Wantage, she was the first to disappear in 2007. This is a real bummer she was a single mother bringing up her seven year-old son alone after the death of her soldier husband in Afghanistan in 2006. She was reported missing by her father, who'd received a distraught call from his grandson saying that his mum wasn't at home when he came down for breakfast. The boy has lived with his grandparents since then and understandably we get the weekly phone call from the grandfather wanting information that we don't have to give.

Moving along, this is Emma Payne aged 33 from Pangbourne. A divorcee living alone, she disappeared in October 2007, reported missing by a colleague. She was supposed to give the woman a lift to work that day but didn't turn up. Next Sally Fredericks aged 42 from Didcot, went missing April 2008. She was married with one daughter who was away at University in Bath. The husband worked nights as a security guard. Then Donna Clayton spinster aged 35 from Chieveley disappeared at the beginning of November 2008 reported missing by her milkman.

Just six months ago Ellen Hopkins aged 37 from Compton Village, had an on/off relationship with a married man, her mother reported her missing after she was unable to contact her by phone, and now the latest victim one Laura Marks aged 32 from here in Newbury."

Mo pointed to photographs on the wall behind her as she spoke.
"Only one of the women, Sally, was over 40. According to friends and family she didn't look her age and could have easily been mistaken for someone ten years younger. So he targets women he thinks are in their thirties, women who live within a twenty mile radius of Newbury and women who bear a striking resemblance to each other and, as we've recently discovered, to a woman named Isabelle Berriman deceased.

To date we've been unlucky, no information, no clues but after the media release of Laura's photo and the witness information, we seem to be getting feedback from the public at last and hopefully it will lead to an early arrest."

A loud cheer rang round the room and everyone started to

clap.

"Okay hush up now", said Jake "we still have to find and identify this bastard. As I said earlier the Bishops have alerted us to Harry Berriman junior and the photograph of his mother that prompted them to get in touch. Unfortunately the photograph was lost so we have to rely on the Bishops' memory. Harry Berriman was last heard of in Oz and Jacko's checking to see if he's still there and, as you heard, he's also working on the whereabouts of Harry senior.

The witness reports of the car seen nearby and the man entering the block of flats on Salter Street at the approximate time of the abduction are positive leads so let's get this investigation out of the doldrums where it has sat for the last two plus years.

We don't have a report from forensics yet but it's unlikely that he left any clues at the flat. He's been meticulous so far and there's no reason to suspect he'll be sloppy this time."

Mo stood up again.

"DCI Summers wants another meeting here tomorrow at 9am, in the meantime any relevant info pass it on. Don't just sit on it until tomorrow's meeting. Time is of the essence, a breakthrough could save Laura Marks' life. So we need to know any details however trivial as they're gathered."

22

Chapelgate, July 31st 2006

Harry and Penny were enjoying a cup of coffee in the Orangery, overlooking their back garden, when the front door bell rang.

"I'll go" she said.

She opened the door and standing on the doorstep was a man probably in his late twenties about six feet tall with dark brown almost black hair. He had unusual piercing blue eyes, his best feature or maybe his worst. The eyes were cold and restless darting around unable to make direct contact with hers.

"Yes?" asked Penny.

"Hi, I'm looking for Harry Berriman. Do I have the right house?"

"You do. I'm his wife, how can we help you?"

"Oh, so you're the woman who stole him away from my Mother, I expected someone prettier. Well I'm the son he abandoned when he ran off with you ok. Harry's the name, don't suppose you thought we'd ever come face to face eh?"

Penny was stunned, she hadn't expected Harry's son to like her but there was no mistaking the venom in his voice and

92

the hatred in his eyes. She felt her blood run cold.

"You'd better come inside then Harry, he'll be surprised to see you."

"I bet he will" he said, as he followed Penny though the dining room and into the Orangery.

His father turned and smiled as they came in.

"Oh we have visitors."

"No it's family coming to call. Hello Dad, long time no see."

"Harry? How did you find us? How are you, son? How's your mother?"

"So many questions Dad, then that's hardly surprising after 20 years," he replied sarcastically.

"So in answer, one it wasn't easy but I was determined. Two I'm fine no thanks to you and three she went crazy and killed herself. Anyway if you married her" he said, inclining his head toward Penny "you must know she's dead."

"Penny and I aren't actually married, we just call ourselves husband and wife. I had no idea that your mother was either crazy or dead and I'm sorry to hear it. So what happened to you after she died? No-one bothered to get in touch with me."

"No one knew or cared where you were. I spent years in an orphanage thanks to you and your fancy woman. The only thing I had left was this poxy photograph of our, so called, perfect family."

Harry threw the picture at his father. Picking it up his father looked at the smiling faces staring back at him.

"I understand your anger, Harry" he said, "and I can only apologise. If I'd known about your mother we'd have gladly given you a home. Wouldn't we Pen?"

"Yes, of course we would" she said, unconvincingly. She'd taken an instant dislike to Harry's son.

"Now you have found us I hope you'll stick around. It would be nice to build bridges and get to know each other again."

"I'd really like that Dad. Sorry for the outburst, years of frustration and resentment making me crabby". His tone no longer confrontational, in fact, was almost friendly.
"How did you get here?"
"Drove, the car's parked outside the gates. I work in Newbury as a Paramedic and I'm renting a place nearby. I transferred there from Manchester about three months ago when I found out you were living in the area."

"I hope we can persuade you to stay for lunch", said Harry, overjoyed to see his son after so many years. "I'm sure Penny can make the lamb stretch to feed another mouth. She's always managed to accommodate unexpected guests before, haven't you love?"

Penny groaned inwardly. The change in his attitude hadn't fooled her. He was an angry young man that was blatantly obvious. What did he really want from them? But she smiled and said "always room for another at our table."
"Thanks I'd love to stay."
"That's settled then" said Harry standing up. "Let's get that car of yours off the road and onto the driveway."
"Ok Dad, lead on" his son said amiably. "Thanks for making me welcome and please forgive my rudeness earlier"

He turned to Penny and smiled but the smile didn't reach those hostile blue eyes. She watched them leave and felt a real sense of foreboding.

23

Newbury, 2009

Although Jake had spent most of the day thinking about the case, what they knew and, more to the point, what they didn't know, every now and then his mind strayed to the lovely Jaime. Unconsciously he picked up his mobile and dialled Mo's house number. It rang several times before a breathless Jaime answered it.

"I'm afraid Jess and Mo are unavailable. Can I take a message?" The breathlessness made her voice sound sexy and Jake felt himself responding in a way that surprised him.

"Hi Jaime, its Jake Summers, just wondering if you'd had a change of heart about that date?"

"Why would I? Never dated a cop yet and I see no reason to change that resolve." Any feeling of desire was immediately quashed by her annoyed response.

"Okay, okay just thought I'd check. My real reason for ringing is that I heard on the grapevine that you worked with Gus Harrison. Do any profiling yourself?'

"Mo's been talking again!" she said. "Yes I've worked with Gus a few times but I'm no expert."

"I thought maybe you could help us get an insight into the character of this guy who's plucking women from their homes", said Jake.

"Sorry I snapped, just getting cranky with some writing issues", she replied.

"I didn't mean to disturb you."

"You didn't really; in fact it's probably good that you rang. I needed a reason to leave well alone until some inspiration returns."

"So will you give this character profile a go?"

"How much do the police pay a lapsed forensic psychologist? Only joking, I'll help if I can but don't expect miracles, I'm no Gus Harrison. Come over tonight and bring the case notes with you. Jess and Mo are off to the theatre so we'll have the place to ourselves."

"Sounds perfect, I'll order a Pizza and bring wine. We can review the case at the same time."

"This still isn't a date DCI Summers."

"I wouldn't assume otherwise but we still need to eat."

"As long as you realise that. I'll see you later", laughed Jaime.

Jake was smiling as he put down the phone.

"You look happy Guv", said Jacko when he popped his head round Jake's open door. "Solved the case already?"

"I wish", Jake sighed.

"I have news on Berriman senior. It seems he and his wife have a villa on the outskirts of Lagos in Portugal and according to my sources they're in residence there now. They also own a rather grand place near the village of East Ilsley, only a 15-minute drive from Newbury. I have a phone number for them in Portugal. Do you want to contact them?"

"Put it on file for now Jacko, we don't want to stir up a hornet's nest until we know if sonny boy is in this country. If he's still in Oz we'll have to think again", replied Jake.

"I'm onto that one too Guv. I'm just waiting for a reply from Senior Sergeant Will Green an officer in the Victoria Police Force. We worked together on a case when I was in Liverpool with the Merseyside Force. He helped us crack a drugs operation that had tentacles stretching as far as Melbourne and Bangkok. Great guy, a real terrier, so if

Berriman junior is in Melbourne no doubt Will will track him down."

"Thanks Jacko, keep up the good work. It sounds promising though with the Berrimans living so close."

"What looks promising, Guv?" Mo asked, catching the tail end of their conversation.

"Jacko's turning up some good stuff", said Jake.

"And, hopefully, I'm off to turn up some more" Jacko said, as he left the office.

Five minutes later Jake had brought Mo up to speed with the new information.

"Wonder how much time they spend in Portugal? Could be a great opportunity for the son to make use of the family home in East Ilsley. Sounds absolutely perfect, isolated, in fact just the place for stashing his victims", said Mo.

"I think you're jumping the gun a bit Mo. We're on the same wavelength though I think the expression is great minds think alike."

"It could break this case wide open if Berriman is living in the UK now", Mo said, excitedly.

"Whoa there, I don't want to build our hopes up too much only to have them dashed later when we find out he's alive and well in Oz."

"Okay, but hey you can't blame a girl for feeling optimistic for the first time in a very long time. Anyway I came in to ask if I can get off half hour early tonight. Our third anniversary already, I can't believe it. Jess has booked seats at the Watermill Theatre for a whodunit and we're dining Italian in Newbury beforehand. I'll get in early tomorrow to prepare for the meeting."

"A whodunit" Jake laughed, "really Mo, surely you've had enough of crime scenes without spoiling your leisure time with another. One consolation tonight is they'll solve the case in a couple of hours."

"So the half hour is it okay?" Mo smiled.

"Sure thing, you always put in more hours than you should anyway."

"Thanks. Goodnight, see you tomorrow."

"Shut the door behind you please, I want some quiet time to get my thoughts together before tomorrow." What he meant was 'before I discuss it with Jaime tonight'.

24

Chapelgate

Laura knew she was about to drown. Unable to move, her arms trapped beneath the rope that bound her to the pillar and the water already up to her chin and rising. And still it gushed in through the 10inch diameter pipe in the wall. She began to panic trying desperately to struggle free from the bonds that held her fast. Her breathing accelerated and, although the water was cold, beads of sweat broke out on her forehead. She thought of her mother. Her own rebellious teenage years when she'd deliberately antagonised her mother. Why had she been such a cow? Effectively they'd been estranged since, nothing more than indifference between them. Remembering those wasted years she felt the tears welling up in her eyes. Too late to say she was sorry. No chance now for reconciliation. She thought of Dan. Wished he were there so she could forgive him, tell him she loved him and make everything right in their world. The water had reached her bottom lip, her heart was pounding and her pulses racing. She was so cold. Shivering uncontrollably she wanted it to be over. She closed her eyes and resigned herself to death by drowning.

A loud noise, like a clap of thunder, woke her and startled

she realised that she'd been dreaming. She was cold because the blanket covering her had slipped off and knocked the glass of water over onto the mattress and she was lying in the wet patch it had made. She turned her head, saw him sitting there silently watching her, and screamed.

"Bad dream Mommie Dearest?" he asked, smiling. She was still shivering.

"A nightmare, but then being trapped here against my will is just as much a nightmare" she said, with a shaky voice.

"Entirely your own fault, you should have treated me better when you had the chance."

She flung herself down on the mattress and, turning her back on him, began to sob helplessly, knowing she was held firm in the grasp of a mad man. He watched silently and waited. Waited for the tears that wracked her body to dwindle and die.

The emotional melt down lasted ten minutes before Laura began to focus. This was what he wanted to do, instil fear and watch as she disintegrated into a gibbering wreck. He probably got off on the power it gave him. She sat up and turned towards him glaring.

"Still here then?" she said, defiantly.

"Still here" he answered. "First the tears then the anger; you do know that nothing will change my plans for you Mommie Dearest."

"Which are?"

"Let's just say I want you to enjoy my hospitality for a while."

"And then what? Are you going to release me? "

"Release you", he laughed out loud, "how can I possibly release you? You know who I am and you know why you're here. Releasing you would make me one stupid man."

"So you're going to kill me?" She could feel her resolve not to show fear rapidly diminishing.

"I'd rather say punish you."

"For what? I keep telling you I've never set eyes on you

before you turned up at the flat pretending to be a Paramedic."

"How's the nose?" he asked, ignoring her outburst.

Thrown by his sudden concern and conversational tone she gingerly touched her nose and yes it did feel much better.

"It's improving" she said, reluctantly.

"Good, any breathing difficulties would spoil my plans for you. No pretence by the way I am a bona fide Paramedic."

"Aren't you supposed to help people?"

"I can and have on many occasions but then my skills can be turned to many things. Subduing and sedating you for example made your abduction and transfer here a smooth and silent one."

"Where is here?"

"You really do belabour a point. As I said before you don't need to know, but don't worry it's somewhere no one will think of looking. Just you and me miles from anywhere."

The laugh that followed was pure evil and more terrifying than all his verbal threats. She felt involuntary shivers course down her spine and her body began to shake as he continued to laugh maniacally. It stopped as suddenly as it began.

"Sorry, getting carried away by visualising the impossible predicament you now find yourself in" he said, in a cold detached way that was completely void of emotion.

She retrieved the blanket and pulled it up round her neck not wanting him to see the uncontrollable responses of her body that betrayed her fear. He stared at her for what seemed an eternity before he pointed to the wet patch on the mattress.

"Try and be more careful with the water from now on" he said, and then he turned and left.

Alone she gave into the tears that shook her until once again she fell into a restless sleep.

25

Carlton Police Station, Melbourne, Australia

"Just had a request from a mate in the Thames Valley Police Force in the UK Sir", Will Green addressed his boss, Chief Inspector Steve Hollins.

"I worked with him on that drugs bust case in Liverpool a couple of years ago. Seems they have a series of abductions spanning the last 30-months in the Newbury area of Berkshire. At this stage it's not an official request. He'd like to locate a Harry Berriman, last heard of about 8-years ago here in Melbourne. They are interested in his whereabouts so they can make it official or cross him off their suspect list. We've just wrapped up that auto theft case and there's nothing too pressing at the moment, so is it okay if I spend a few hours checking this fella out?"

"Sure, go ahead Will. We need to cultivate good relations with overseas forces, we may need their help some day."

"Thanks Sir, I'll let you know the outcome."

Will headed back to his desk and turned on his lap top. First search plumbing firms in Melbourne. It was too much to hope for Berriman Plumbing Co to feature. No luck, so many plumbing companies and not a Berriman plumbing to be seen. Okay so now check LinkedIn for Berrimans in business, five hits and there he was:

Harry Berriman - Owner, Plumbing Solutions, Abbotsford, Melbourne Victoria.

Will was chuffed that it had been so easy, he picked up White Pages and looked up the Plumbing Solutions phone number. A couple of minutes later he had dialled the number and a female answered.

"Plumbing Solutions, how can we help?"

"Hi, I'm Senior Sergeant Green from Carlton Police, I was wondering if I could speak to Mr Harry Berriman?"

"Sorry Harry's not in today."

"It's quite important that I speak with him as soon as possible. Can you tell me how I can reach him?"

"No chance, you're just a voice on the end of a phone. I don't give personal information out to just anyone."

"Appreciate that Mam, just phone Carlton Police Station and ask for me, Senior Sergeant Will Green."

"I'll do that" she said, and abruptly rang off.

His phone rang minutes later. It was Donna Ives, one of the police support staff.

"A Mrs Donaldson, from a company called Plumbing Solutions, is on the blower for you Will. You got a leaky pipe mate?"

He didn't have to see her face to imagine the big grin that was spread across it.

"Cheeky, just put her through will you."

"Sure, Mrs Donaldson for you Sergeant Green."

"So Sergeant Green, you really do exist. Ok, as you've proved to be kosher you'll find Mr Berriman at his home. His number is 9312 7660."

"Thanks for your cooperation Mam. I'll ring him now."

Green spent several minutes talking to Berriman's wife Elizabeth. Harry was out playing golf and wouldn't be back for a couple of hours at least. So Will arranged to drop round that afternoon for a chat with Harry. Obviously Elizabeth was curious but he didn't tell her too much, just that it was a matter concerning Harry's family back in the UK, which made her even more curious.

"He doesn't have family back in the UK", she said.

"Maybe you're right but I just need to check a few things with him anyway. Thank you Mrs Berriman" and he put the phone down quickly before she could ask any more questions.

After lunch, and before leaving the station, Will told Leading Senior Constable Josh Harman his plans.

"If anyone's looking for me I'm on my way to Hampton Park, No 5 Cheney Avenue to be precise."

"You going up in the world Sergeant Green? That's a very classy area" Harman replied.

"Yeah plumbers must be earning megabucks now" Green said, laughing.

"More than us mere constables that's for sure."

Hampton Park was certainly one of the better suburbs of Melbourne. Will pulled up outside 5 Cheney Avenue and a 'wow, that's impressive' escaped his lips. He was looking at a large single story home with double garage, open sided, covered car port and a large frontage laid to grass and surrounded by flowering shrubs, the whole encompassed by ornate white railings. Will let out a low whistle and thought must be worth $600,000 +, not bad for a'''Pommie' plumber. Then he muttered 'Will that was uncalled for, he's probably worked hard for his money and is one of the good guys.'

He walked up to the front door and rang the bell. An attractive brunette, probably in her mid to late twenties, opened the door.

"Oh", she said, seeing Will in uniform, "you must be Sergeant Green, come in we've been expecting you. Harry's out in the back yard having a kick around with our 3-year-old. Do you want to speak to him in here or out in the yard?"

"Probably best in here Mam."

"Fine, I'll show you into the study. Make yourself

comfortable I'll send him in."

Will glanced out of the window which overlooked the backyard. He saw a young man about 30 kicking a large colourful ball and a small blonde haired boy running around frantically and laughing. The man was slim, looked fairly muscular, and was probably around 1.8 m tall. A mop of unruly dark hair flopped over his forehead and a happy smile lit his handsome face. The yard was large, probably about 2000sq m Will estimated, and was beautifully landscaped. A decking area directly behind the house had steps down to a circular lawn where Liz had just joined the other two and was talking to the man he assumed was Harry. To the left of the lawn a paved area with a large covered pergola housed a barbie and some very classy garden furniture. There were flowering plants everywhere. To the right of the lawn a tree-lined walkway led to another area with a summerhouse that obscured the rest of the view. Wow, I was right; this place must have cost a fortune. Plumbing must be a lucrative business these days, Will thought. He watched as Liz scooped the youngster up in her arms and then she and Harry walked towards the house.

Harry came into the study, shook hands with Will and introduced himself.
"Harry Berriman, Brit by birth, Australian by choice. I'm 29-years-old, been here almost a third of my life, have my own successful plumbing business which I started from scratch, married my beautiful wife Elizabeth four years ago. We have two children, Benjamin three and Ellie just 10-months, and we moved to Hampton Park 18-months ago. I have never knowingly broken the law so how can I help you Sergeant?"

Will couldn't help smiling, the young man still sounded very English and very proper.
"Well, sounds fair dinkum to me Harry, however I do need ask you a few questions. Been back to the UK within in

the last 3 years?"

"No never felt the need."

"Any proof?" Will asked.

"Sure, ask any of my blokes at work, I never take more than a few days off at a time, too busy building up the business. Liz can vouch for that too. Why would I want to go back? My family and my business are here. Look what's this all about, why do you need to know my whereabouts anyway?"

"Just following up an inquiry from the Thames Valley Force in England", said Will. "Apparently over the last couple of years several women have been snatched from their homes, the latest just a few days ago. A Jenny and Rob Bishop called in saying the woman bore a remarkable likeness to your mother, Isabelle Berriman."

"How would they know, they never met her and she's been dead for years", replied Harry.

"Yes, true, but they mentioned you kept a photo of you mother with you as a boy, and they recognised a likeness to the missing woman."

"I lost that photo about a year after I went to Stirling House."

"They told the police that too. Anyway, the circumstances surrounding your arrival at Stirling House, the missing women resembling your mother and the fact that your father now lives in that area gave them cause for concern."

"You mean they thought I was involved in their disappearance?" Harry asked.

"Well, it was one line of inquiry and they all have to be followed up. Thankfully I can verify that you're here in Australia, so that particular line of inquiry ends now. Thank you for your time", said Will .

"Not so fast, you said my father lives in the area. What area?"

"Berkshire."

"More specifically?"

"Newbury area."

"My God, only a few miles from where I last saw him. Does he know I'm here in Oz? Come to that does he even care? He certainly didn't when he left us 20-years ago", said Harry.

"Sorry, I only know about the case on a need-to-know basis, no more and no less. Do you want me to ask them to get in touch with you so you can ask for details?" asked Will .

"Why not, Dad owes me a few explanations."

"Give me your Email address then and I'll pass it on."

Harry walked over to his desk, wrote it down and then handed it to Will.

"Thanks Sergeant Green. I appreciate that."

"Ok Mr Berriman, then I'm out of here. Glad you're not involved" he said as he shook Harry's hand. And he was, the earnest young man had impressed Will with his straight-talking. Australia needed young men like Harry, honest and hard-working.

As he unlocked the car a thought struck him. He turned round, went back and rang the bell.

"Back so soon?" Harry said, as he answered the door smiling.

"Sorry to disturb you again but could I have a photograph so that people in the UK can actually identify you as the Harry Berriman they know."

"Very thorough sergeant, you're right of course anyone can steal an identity these days. Come to the office I'll print one for you."

Will followed him back into the office and watched as Harry switched on his PC and put two sheets of photographic paper into the printer. After several minutes the printer produced two quality photographs. Harry handed one to Will, took the other and started to write something on the back of it. Will looked at the happy family scene.

"That was taken outside the Visitors Centre at Bundoora Park about a year ago", said Harry glancing up. "Mother-in-law did the honours."

A grinning Harry held Ben close to his chest in the crook

of his right arm and his left arm encompassed the shoulders of his heavily pregnant wife.

"Nice picture" said Will.

"Yeah, I've printed another for Janet and Rob Bishop to keep. I've just written a short note on the back of that one. Perhaps you'll scan both sides before you send it so they get the message."

"Sure thing and thanks, you've been very co-operative."

"Nothing to hide sergeant, nothing to hide", Harry replied, smiling.

As Will walked to his car he read the brief note that Harry had scribbled.

To Jenny and Rob
I will always remember your kindness. As you see I have my own family now. The bump became my daughter Ellie 10-months ago and my son Ben is now a happy 3-year old.
Harry

Will smiled, got in his car and drove back to the station.

26

Croft Cottage, 7.00pm

Jake rang the bell and waited. It was a while before the door was opened by a smiling Jaime leaning on crutches.

"An Inspector calls", she said.

"Very droll," said Jake laughing.

"Sorry it took me so long to answer but it's not easy getting around on these" she said, waving one of the crutches at him.

"So are you letting me in or am I being kept on the doorstep?"

"Come in. I never keep people bearing gifts, particularly a good red, on the doorstep."

"Pizza will arrive about 7:30pm. I've ordered a Margherita and a Chicago style, ok?" he asked, following her through the kitchen into the sitting room.

"Chicago style eh? So you do think I'm a gangster?" she said, as she turned to look at him and then flopped down in the armchair by the fire.

"Sit down" she said, pointing to the nearby settee. "On second thoughts, go open the wine. Glasses are in the cupboard by the fridge."

He came back carrying one large and one small glass of Rioja, handed her the large one and sat down on the settee and raised his glass.

"Cheers."

"Too many of these and any profiling skills I might have will fly out the window", she said, as she raised her glass too.

"Did you bring case notes?"

"No it's all in here" he said, tapping his head "but let's wait until we've eaten before we talk shop."

"I didn't mention you coming here to Mo or Jess. I wasn't sure if you wanted them to know."

"I didn't say anything to Mo either, I just wanted to see if you could give us any insight before I did."

"Avoid the ribbing you'd get for coming over here two nights on the trot more like."

"Ok you've tumbled me, satisfied?" Jake smiled, and made Jaime laugh.

"Go get the pizza Summers", said Jaime, as the doorbell rang. "The cutter and cutlery are in the drawer under the hob and the plates in the cupboard to the left of it. Oh and there's a salad in the fridge."

"Ever thought of joining the army? You'd make a splendid Sergeant Major."

She laughed again as he went to do her bidding coming back several minutes later with two sliced pizzas and a bowl of full of salad, plates and cutlery all of which he placed on the coffee table between them.

"Now I expect you want me to serve it Mam?"

"Great idea, I'll settle for a slice of each and some salad please."

They chatted amiably throughout the meal, nothing forced, all very relaxed and Jaime thought perhaps I should give him a chance. However, she didn't voice her thoughts and refused a second glass of wine.

"Shall we make a start then?" she said, "We only have about four hours before the happy couple return from their night out."

Jake spent the next couple of hours going over case details with her, sticking rigidly to the facts and careful not to influence her in any way with theories or suspect details. She asked a few questions and took detailed notes.

"Ok, now I need some quiet time to think about this", she said, finally. "Leave it with me and I'll get back to you if and when I can give you something concrete to work with."

"Are you giving me my marching orders?"

"Afraid so", she nodded, "but if you don't want them to know you've been here detective, one set of dishes need washing, the remains of one pizza put in the fridge, the other needs dumping so take it with you and, a cup of coffee, white one sugar, would be nice before you leave."

"This isn't even a date lady and now I know why, you don't date men you just want them at your beck and call."

"Got it in one Jake, now I know why you're a detective."

He went to the kitchen, did the jobs he'd been assigned and returned with her coffee.

"Well I'll get off then" and before she could object bent and kissed her cheek.

"Round one to me and I look forward to round two" he smiled.

"You took advantage of a helpless woman" but her smile told him she really didn't mind too much. "I won't get up."

"Didn't think you would, ladies don't usually stand when they dismiss their man servants" he said, as he strode from the room.

She heard the front door shut and then he was gone and she was sorry. She liked Jake Summers, perhaps a little too much.

She hobbled into her room, sat at the makeshift desk and started work on the profile. About midnight she heard Mo and Jess come in so she made her way into the sitting room.

"Have a good time?" she asked.

"Wonderful" said Jess, ecstatically. "Miss Marple here solved it in 5-minutes flat, but we enjoyed it didn't we babes?"

"The food was good", Mo nodded, "the company was good and I solved the crime, what more could anyone want?"

"So what have you been up to sister mine?" asked Jess.

"Mostly working but I did order a pizza like I said I would, there's some left in the fridge if you're still hungry."

"After all that pasta, not a chance, no doubt Mo will take some to work tomorrow she just loves cold pizza."

"Glad you had a good time. Think I'll hit the sack now, goodnight."

"Goodnight" they said in unison.

"I always said we were good together", Mo giggled.

And they were. From the moment she'd met Jess in Reading, more specifically in one of the premier gay clubs in the Thames Valley just three years ago, she'd known how good they'd be together. The attraction was immediate but it took Mo three months to persuade Jess to sleep with her, to convince her that she wasn't a one night stand type of girl and was interested only in a loving, long term relationship. But boy was the wait worth it, the sex was indescribably good and within months they were living together in Newbury, where they both worked.

Mo looked at her beautiful partner.

"I think hitting the sack is a very good idea. I know the perfect way to end a perfect evening", she said, taking Jess's hand and leading her upstairs to their bedroom.

27

Chapelgate

The door to the cellar was thrown open and Laura watched as her captor struggled down the steps backwards dragging something down with him. She started to sob uncontrollably when she finally saw the white wooden coffin he'd placed in front of her.

"Why so sad Mommie Dearest? This is your new home."

He opened the lid; the inside was padded and lined with white satin. A white satin pillow and gown completed the interior. He shut the lid again and pointing to the clear, acrylic tube that was inserted into the lid of the coffin.
"I can pump air to you through this pipe even when you're underground. It was invented over a hundred years ago by Mr William White who called it the safest coffin in the world. But then the distressed occupant received air until they were rescued. You, Mommie Dearest, will receive air until I decide otherwise."
"I don't give a stuff who invented the bloody thing, only a monster like you could think of using it."

Ignoring the outburst he continued to describe the fate that would befall her.

"Once the tube is sealed you have about an hour before you asphyxiate. Time to reflect on how bad a mother you were. I'll help you move in tomorrow."

And then he was gone.
"You crazy bastard" she shouted after him. "Why are you doing this, I don't even know you."

Realising the futility of her actions she stopped shouting and sobbing and started to concentrate on a way to escape. She examined the shackles that bound her to the pillar. She'd done this a dozen times before but to no avail. Perhaps this time she'd see some way to free herself. The metal band securing her ankle to the chain was made from two semi-circles of iron held together with thick brass padlocks. The free end of the chain had been wrapped around the pillar and secured with a heavy duty 10-digit combination lock which had made her scream in frustration as she'd punched in one set of numbers after another without success. Think logically, Laura, think, what numbers are meaningful to him.
"How the hell should I know," she screamed loudly.

Freedom is just ten numbers away. Then it hit her, what did he always say "Mommie Dearest." She started to count, M was the 13th letter of the alphabet, O the 15th and, oh my God, she had a ten digit number after taking all the letters of Mommie. 1315131395. She punched it in, nothing, the lock held fast.
'Bugger, bugger, bugger', she thought, 'is it worth trying Dearest? Probably not but I'll give it a go'. Again she came up with a 10-digit number 4511851920. She punched it in, bingo the lock sprung open. Hardly able to contain her excitement she pulled the chain free from the pillar and, picking it up so it didn't drag behind her, hurried over to the work bench. She chose her weapon carefully unhooking a large wooden mallet she thought would be perfect to knock his block off. She knew he would bring food in a couple of hours, she would wait impatiently. 'I'm

ready now', she thought, 'bring it on'

.

28

Chapelgate

She heard the door open and watched as he walked down cellar steps carrying a tray with food and, oh my God, he'd brought wine. He stopped by the bench and put the tray down.
'What the hell is he doing' thought Laura. She was on the mattress as usual, the unsecured chain still wrapped round the pillar, the mallet was covered by a blanket close to her hand, surely he couldn't see anything amiss.

He stood silently by the bench staring at her and then he smiled.
"I've brought wine to celebrate Mommie Dearest", he said. "I thought Dad was the clever one but you've excelled all expectations."
'He knows' Laura thought, 'how the hell can he know?'
"See the smoke detectors over the bench here", he said, as if he could read her thoughts, "and by your pillar, well they are wireless CCTV cameras and guess what? They send pictures to my PC upstairs."

Unexpectedly he started to sing 'Every breath you take, every move you make, every bond you break, every step you take, I'll be watching you.'

"Ironic really, a Police hit, remember that do you?"

Laura was chilled to the bone.
"Ok, so you know, but I still have this", she said, defiantly as she pulled the mallet from its hiding place and stood up trying to look threatening.
"Come any closer and I'll use it."
"Now I'm really scared" he said, mocking her by knocking his knees together.
"You should be you bastard" she said, with bravado she didn't feel.

Laughing, he pulled a gun from the back of his trouser waist band and pointed it at her.
"Put it down or I'll blow your head off and end it now."
"Go ahead, better that than being buried alive."
"I'm sure you'd much rather play the game. A few more days to live, to think of another escape plan maybe or to be rescued by the gallant Jake Summers."
"Who the hell is Jake Summers?" asked Laura.
"The DCI in charge of your case, but then you wouldn't know that, would you? You've been locked up here, so you haven't seen the news. Well Jake and his team, probably the whole Thames Valley Force, are searching for you as we speak. So what about it? Are you putting that thing down" he said, waving the gun towards the mallet "or do I pull the trigger?"
"Bastard!" exclaimed Laura, as she threw the mallet down.
"But you know that's not true, you and Dad were married when I was conceived" he said, angrily. "Kick the mallet over here and sit down."

Resigned, Laura kicked the mallet towards him and flopped down onto the mattress.
"That's better" he said, picking something up from the tray and walking towards her.
When he reached the mallet he kicked it backwards and further out of her reach. Then he showed her the padlock he was holding.

"Completely tamper proof just like the ones on your ankle, no more combination locks, you're far too clever for those." He moved behind her and re-secured the chain.

"There" he said, smiling "glass of wine with your meal?"

"Drink with you, never! I only drink with friends and family and you're no friend and certainly not family. By the way, if I really was your mother I'd have drowned you at birth."

"True colours coming out now Mommie Dearest" he said, picking up the tray "don't suppose you want my food either." With that retort he left her hungry and alone.

"Go to hell" she shouted after him as hunger pangs gripped her stomach.

29

Newbury Police Station, 8:30 am

Jake sat down in his office and within minutes Jacko was knocking on his door.

"Come in" he looked up expectantly.

"Bad news I'm afraid Guv", Jacko shook his head. "Email from Will Green waiting for me when I got in. To cut a long story short, Harry Berriman junior is alive and well and living in the Melbourne suburbs with his wife and kids. He's been in Oz for the last nine years or so, never been back to Blighty and has no plans to do so. Will also sent a couple of photos of Harry so we can get a positive ID from the Bishops."

"Sod it, bang goes that theory. I really thought we had a viable suspect."

"Sorry Guv" said Jacko, sympathetically. "Oh and before I go, Berriman had no idea his father was back in the UK, gave Will his Email address and asked if we could give him any details, maybe an address or phone number for his Dad."

"Leave that to you then Jacko, get in touch with Berriman senior and tell him we've located his son in Australia and ask him if he wants us to pass on any details to him."

"So what explanation do I give when he asks me how I happen to have his phone number and how we knew his son was in Oz.?"

"I'm sure you'll think of something, you're a bright boy Jacko. See you at the meeting."

"Thanks Guv" he said, sarcastically.

"Pleasure. Oh and Jacko, don't give too much away when you get in touch with Berriman senior. Oh and can you tell DS Connolly I'd like a word."

Jacko left muttering something about a broom and his backside. Jake had to smile although he had nothing to smile about.

"I gather from the look on Jacko's face the Australian connection didn't pan out" Mo said, as she walked into his office.

"No, yet another dead end, damn it. Any more good news before we go into the meeting?"

"Well only that Uniform has interviewed everyone in Laura's block and no one works in the Ambulance Service. In fact no one anywhere in the area works in the Ambulance Service. No one admits to calling for an ambulance. Only one NHS worker. She lives in the next block and works out of the Northcroft Surgery as a district nurse."

"Sounds promising. This so called Paramedic could be our man then. Firstly, we now know he doesn't live in Laura Marks's block of flats. Secondly, he was seen there at the right time on the day she disappeared. And finally there's no known reason for his being there. Would you trust a Paramedic and invite him into your home Mo?"

"Probably, depends what reason he gave for ringing my doorbell, if it was plausible yes I'd let him in."

"Exactly, but are we really looking for a Paramedic. Or, are we looking for a man dressed as one for the purpose of deception and abduction?"

"Your guess is as good as mine", Mo shrugged.

"Right, after the meeting take Gregg and get down to the Ambulance Station on Oxford Road. If he is in the Service and works out of Newbury we may get lucky."

The phone rang then so Mo gave him the thumbs up and left. As he picked up he saw Mo walk over to Gregg's desk.

"Hi Jake, it's me." He recognised Jaime's voice immediately. "I have a sketchy profile for you, not very detailed I'm afraid but then we don't have that much information to go on do we?"

"My God you did that quickly, you must have worked on it all night."

"Pretty much, when I get my teeth into something I just don't quit at midnight. Do you want me to Email it to you?"

"That would be great, send it to my personal account jakesummers@tagmail.com. And thank you. I'll be in touch."

"I'm sure you will" she said, and put the phone down. He opened his Email account and waited. A couple of minutes later he was reading it.

Offender Profile
The offender is a white male aged between 25 and 35.
He is intelligent and solitary but sociable enough to pull off adult female abductions by gaining easy access to their homes.
May do this by adopting a trustworthy persona e.g. a priest or policeman.
A violent, repetitive offender often exhibits another element of criminal behaviour during the crime - the signature aspect or 'calling card.' This criminal conduct is a unique and integral part of the offender's behaviour and goes beyond the actions needed to commit the crime.
His crime scene signature or 'calling card' is 'Mommie Dearest' which suggests that he suffered abuse at the hands of his mother resulting in a dysfunctional relationship between mother and son.
The abductions are probably more to do with revenge than sex, control or power.

Abductees are all lookalikes, same age, same race and same physical type. They probably share these characteristics with the abuser.

Likely to subject his victims to the same or similar abuse that he suffered.

Could keep his victims alive for a time but death is the ultimate revenge.

Time between abductions is probably determined more by the availability of his holding facility rather than an infrequent desire to commit the crime.

The first abduction could have been as the result of an accidental sighting of a woman that reminded him of his mother. Until that moment he could have thought she was dead. That sighting triggered his desire for revenge and to punish the 'mother' for the childhood abuse.

It was more than revenge though; he actually found the experience satisfying and enjoyable.

However, after that first enjoyable experience, he now actively searches for lookalikes. This allows him licence to repeat the offence and furthermore, justification for committing the crime. After identifying a victim he follows them, familiarises himself with their lives and then choses a time when they are alone and vulnerable to abduct them.

A dangerous, well organized offender has access to a vehicle for moving his victims and to drugs to sedate them. He could be someone who works in, or has knowledge of, the medical/veterinary professions.

Exhibits the ritualistic behaviour of a serial offender/killer.

Jake read it twice and was impressed by her profiling skills. She'd done a really good job in a very short time. Her conclusions went along the same lines as their thinking. It was good to have a professional opinion. 'Well done Jaime' he thought.

He Emailed her immediately:

Hi Jaime
Firstly let me say how much I enjoyed our date last night!!! Seriously

thanks for the profile nice to have a professional opinion mirroring most of our thoughts about this guy. I will show it to Mo, she and the others should be made aware of your conclusions. By the way, she gave me a copy of your first novel so I look forward to reading it. Must fly, briefing in a couple of minutes.
See you soon
Jake

He hit the send button.

30

Incident Room

As always the room was crowded and noisy; the crime scene officers were there too, adding to the cacophony of voices. Jake banged loudly on the table to get their attention. It was then he noticed ACC Davis secreted among the uniforms at the back of the room.

"Listen up, we have some bad news and some good news. The bad news is, it seems, Harry Berriman junior is no longer in the frame for this. A colleague on the Melbourne force has checked him out and sure enough he lives in Oz and has been living there for the last nine years. He's never been back to the UK since he emigrated. DC Miller, we have a photo of said Harry Berriman junior, so after we finish up here I want you to get over to Stirling House and get the Bishops to give us a positive ID."

"Will do Guv."

Mo watched Barry Leyland visibly cringe at the use of the word 'Guv'.

"The good news is there are other leads we are following up:

One. As you know a witness reported seeing a man in a green uniform entering the flats on Salter Street around the estimated time of the abduction. Uniformed officers have been checking the flats and surrounding areas. No one wears a green uniform for work. This begs the questions who is he and why was he there? We know that Paramedics wear green uniforms so Sergeant Connolly and DC Gregg will be going down to Oxford Road Ambulance Station from this meeting to see if we can make any headway there.

Two. The car with the mirrored windows. Any joy with that one Dusty?"

Dusty Miller stood up.

"Nothing concrete Guv. Several companies sell adhesive products that transform plain glass into one-way mirrors. Anyone in the car can see out but no one can see in. It's an ingenious way to watch and gather information in a clandestine way without being seen."

"How come this car hasn't been reported before? Something so unusual and highly illegal surely arouses suspicion." A loud voice interjected.

Dusty turned to face Barry Leyland.

"It may not be mirrored the whole time Sir, the adhesive film can be removed and reapplied without too much trouble."

"Have you checked out local suppliers Dusty?" Jake asked.

"Nothing locally really Guv, it's mostly bought on line. It's readily available from places like Amazon and eBay. It's meant to be used for safety purposes, not to be used on cars to protect the identity of people with hidden agendas. Lots of records to check if we go that route Guv."

"If we get desperate we may need to, ok Dusty thanks", said Jake. "I see the crime scene boys are here, anything to tell us Mike?"

"Nothing you want to hear, basically all prints lifted from the flat and the car are, as we predicted, family and friends. Other than a few sets of prints the car was clean so we handed it back to Dan Williams yesterday. We also gave him permission to move back into the flat but he's staying put at Claremont Gardens until Laura's there to quote 'welcome him back.' The blood type found on the floor in

the hallway is O Rh D positive which Laura shares with 37% of the population in the UK so no go there either Sir."
"Just as we thought Mike, he didn't get careless this time either. So, does anyone have any questions or theories that they'd like to share?"

PC Halliday, of the red face and orange hair, stood up.
"What I don't understand Sir, is that according to the Bishops all the abducted women and especially Laura Marks bear a striking resemblance to Isabelle Berriman. Her son was abused and ended up in care so had good reason to hate his mother. Now it seems that all this is just a coincidence, it just doesn't feel right Sir."
Jake was impressed. Halliday might be a rookie PC but his instincts were good.
"Good point Halliday and I couldn't agree more, but at this time we have nowhere to go with this line of inquiry. That said, if there is any connection I'm sure we'll find it.
Anything else? No, ok we'll meet tomorrow after we've checked out the leads I mentioned."
They all filed out looking disappointed.
"We'll get off to Oxford Road now Guv, see you later", said Mo, as she grabbed Gregg.

As they left ACC Davis stood and walked towards Jake. Disappointment clearly etched all over her face too.
"Brick walls in every direction Jake, I was really excited when you told me about Berriman but here we are again no suspects only a shadowy figure in green and a car shrouded in privacy. Not exactly earth shattering news. I think we're still grasping at straws, we're not about to arrest and convict are we?"
"No Mam we're not, but we must cover every angle. But like Halliday, I don't really believe in coincidences. I still think, in fact I'm sure, that there could still be a connection to Isabelle Berriman."
He escorted Helen Davis downstairs and she left with her usual parting shot.
"Keep me informed Jake."

Dead Ringers

31

Ambulance Station, Oxford Road Newbury, 11.30am

Mo drew up outside the Oxford Road Station and, as she and Gregg got out of the car, a man dressed in the green uniform of a Paramedic approached them. He was a tall, muscular man about 50 with a grey crew cut and twinkling blue eyes. 'A bit wrinkled but still handsome' thought Mo.
"Hi, Archie Jenkins, Operational Manager here at Newbury." Mo shook his outstretched hand.
"DS Mo Connolly, DC Gregg, thanks for seeing us."
"Great name Sergeant. Play any tennis yourself?"
"'Fraid not"
"Pity, come upstairs to the office and we'll chat."

Mo and Dave followed him through a side door next to the Ambulance garage area, up a flight of stairs through a staff relaxation area and into a small office. Sitting down behind his desk he pointed to a couple of chairs positioned on the side wall.
"Pull up a pew and sit. How can I help?"
"I suppose like most people you've read about the abductions in our area?" He nodded yes.
"We're here because a witness saw a man in a green uniform entering the block of flats where the latest abduction took place at around the time we think she was

taken."

"And you're thinking one of my men could be responsible."

"It has crossed our minds."

"You do realise that these green uniforms", Jenkins said, patting his own "are readily available on-line and so anyone can buy them. They're not exclusive to the ambulance service."

"No, I didn't", said Mo, "but there is other evidence. We think that the women were drugged in order to remove them quietly from the scene so he must have access to sedatives. Do you carry drugs like that on board the ambulances?"

"No, they are only available in the air ambulance, and are administered by an accompanying doctor, not the crew."

"Do all your staff wear green whistles Officer Jenkins?" Gregg interjected.

"Call me Archie lad, no need to be so formal. The answer is yes and no, the ambulance crews do, and control room staff wear white shirts and dark trousers. The only difference between the ambulance crew is the colour of their epaulettes and that depends on whether they're Paramedics or ECA's." Gregg looked puzzled.

"Emergency Care Assistants."

"Do you always have a crew attending a 999 call?"

"Usually, but we also have motor cycle Paramedics who attend alone. The crews usually consist of two people, a paramedic and an ECA."

"Does any of your staff own an estate car with mirrored windows?"

"Mirrored windows, no I'm pretty sure I would have noticed, in fact I can't even think of a member of staff that owns an estate car. Four-by-four yes, Joe Daley loves his but no estates. I'll ask around to make sure and let you know."

"One last thing,' said Mo "did you receive any 999 calls from Salter Street on the 2nd of November?"

"Don't think so but let's consult the control room staff, they have every call logged." He stood "if you follow me."

They followed him back through the recreation area where two of the staff were watching *Cash in The Attic* on the 42" Widescreen TV, through a fire door into the control room. He introduced them to Senior Control Room Assistant Flick Ashley. She was a small, mousey haired woman in her forties who was wearing large black framed spectacles and a pinched-faced expression. 'Name doesn't suit her' thought Mo. 'Felicity maybe, Flick never.'

"Any calls from Salter Street on November 2nd Flick?" asked Archie.

"I'll look Archie" she said, gazing at him adoringly. Unrequited love was stamped all over her face.

"No, a couple of calls from town stores, a fainting and a heart attack, two RTAs on the A34 and four calls from private houses in the outlying villages. Nothing at all from Salter Street."

"There you go then detectives, no joy, sorry we can't help."

"If you could ask around about the car Archie", said Mo.

"Will do. Is that it then?"

"I guess so" Mo said, getting the distinct impression that they were being dismissed.

"Let me see you out then."

"No need, we can find our own way but thanks again Archie" Mo said, extending her hand.

"Anytime Sergeant, nice to meet you both" Archie said, taking the offered hand and shaking it firmly.

"Well that was a waste of nickel and dime", said Gregg, when they got back in the car.

"Speak English Dave, you can be so irritating", Mo groaned.

"Sorry Sarge, that was a complete waste of time."

"Not necessarily, only time will tell," she grinned at her play on words. Gregg completely missed the point.

"Back to the Station Sarge?"

"Yeah let's go. You can drive."

32

Newbury Police Station

"Get the paperwork done Dave", said Mo, as she and Gregg went straight upstairs. "I'll let DCI Summers know we're back".

Mo knocked on Jake's closed door.
"Come."
Mo went in.
"We're back, no further forward though. The green uniforms are readily available on-line. Sedative drugs are only carried by air ambulance crews so, unless he is air ambulance crew, we don't know how he got them. However, Ketamine is an anaesthetic and is readily available from street dealers. Apparently it's the new recreational drug on the club scene according to Dave Gregg. And he should know he spends enough time in them. This was also backed up by my mate Des Richard, a Sergeant on the Drugs Squad at Reading. He said it was a powerful anaesthetic used mainly by vets but he agreed with Dave it was readily available on the streets too. It's my bet that's what the perp's using."
"Frustrated at every turn", Jake's head dropped into his hands.

At that precise moment Jacko ran in.

"That break, the one you've been looking for Guv, well I think we might just have it", he said excitedly.

"Well don't just stand there man spit it out", said Jake.

"I rang Harry Berriman in Lagos, think I got him out of bed he sounded sleepy. Anyway, I told him we'd located his son in Australia. He didn't even ask me how I got his number or why we'd looked for his son Harry in Oz. In fact he didn't say anything for a moment; I thought we'd been cut off."

Jake clasped his hands and began rhythmically tapping his forefingers together, something he did when he was getting impatient. Mo just leaned forward and put her hand over his to stop him.

"Patience Guv," she said.

"Jacko, I don't think we care whether Berriman was sleepy or asked any questions. What we are interested in is why you're so excited so just get to the point eh."

"Ok, ok I'll cut to the chase. Berriman said his son couldn't possibly be in Australia as he was living with him at Chapelgate, his home near the village of East Ilsley."

Jake stood and clapped Jacko on the back.

"I just got excited too Jacko. So you're telling me we've got two Harry Berrimans?"

"Well, three if you count Harry senior Guv. Yeah, and I almost forgot one other very important fact, the Berrimans go to Lagos twice a year - guess when?"

"April and November?"

"You got it, well almost. They usually leave for Portugal in April, returning at the end of May, then again at the end of October returning a couple of weeks before Christmas. As Berriman said before the tourist season gets into full swing and then again when it's over. They like the quiet life."

"It gets better and better. Stand up the real Harry Berriman. Which one is the imposter?" asked Jake.

"We'll know for sure when Dusty gets back" said Mo, looking over towards his desk.

"In fact any moment now, he just walked in."

Jake went over to the door and beckoned Miller into the office.
"Well, did the Bishops ID Harry Berriman junior?" he asked.
"Yes Guv, he's the real McCoy."
"So who is living at Chapelgate? It's certainly not Harry Berriman Junior! Okay let's get organised. I'll ring Helen Davis; get her authority to bring in an Armed Response Unit. If Harry number two is there in East Ilsley he could be armed. We already know he's dangerous. Mo, ask Inspector Leyland for uniform support, one car should be enough. We'll take Miller and Gregg with us." He picked up the phone.
"Jane, get me ACC Davis, I'll hold."

Moments later Helen Davis came on the line.
"Yes Jake?"
He explained the situation quickly and succinctly.
"I agree, you do need armed support, I'll get that arranged. They should be with you within the hour. Any idea why this guy is pretending to be Harry Berriman?"
"None, Mam, but hopefully we'll soon find out."
"Good luck and, Jake, don't take any unnecessary risks."
"I won't and thank you Mam."

He put down the phone as Mo and Jacko came back into the office. Jacko looked a little sheepish.
"What?" Jake asked worriedly.
"Another thing I forgot to tell you Guv. Berriman said he'd never seen the suspect's car with mirrored windows."
"Pretty irrelevant now wouldn't you say Jacko?" said Jake, feeling relieved it was nothing more serious.
"He probably only did it when they were out of the country. It just made it easier to watch his victims without being seen."
"Has the ACC sanctioned the firearms unit?" Mo asked.
"Yeah an Armed Response Vehicle (ARV) is on its way so

as soon as they get here we'll meet in the Incident Room. In the meantime get our guys kitted out with Kevlar vests and get a couple of squad cars organised. Jacko get back to Berriman senior, we need to know the detailed layout of the house, where the so-called son's room is. How many entrances/exits there are? You know the drill."

"Yes Guv," they said in unison.

33

Forty minutes later Jake was briefing his team, Mo, Gregg, Miller, four uniformed officers, Sergeant Walsh and PCs' Halliday, Talbot and Johnson and the AVR unit consisting of one sergeant and three police constables, all highly trained firearms men. They introduced themselves as Sergeant Gordon and PCs Grimes, Hennessy and Coles.

"Ok this is the situation", said Jake, when the introductions were over. "We have a guy claiming to be a Harry Berriman living at a house near East Ilsley. We have good reason to believe that he is involved in the abduction of six women in our area. He could be armed and dangerous so don't take any risks. The latest victim, Laura Marks, may still be alive so do nothing to endanger her, just tread carefully and follow my lead. Jacko give us the building details."

"Well, according to Harry Berriman Senior his son doesn't actually live in the main house, he has his own place in the grounds. It's located behind a laurel hedge to the left of the landscaped garden. Access to it is through a four-foot gap in the hedge about 20-yards from the building. The entrance is located at the front of the building. To the rear of the building a gravel path leads to the front driveway of the house via a gate in a wall that separates the driveway from the rear garden. The son parks his car, a black five-door Vauxhall Astra Estate, in front of this gateway, in

142

effect blocking access to this area except through the rear garden.

It's a one storey building about 30-metres square that used to be used as a workshop. It does have a cellar beneath it with access at the side of the building facing the hedge. That apparently was used for storage. About three years ago Berriman and his son had the place converted. The top floor became a studio flat."

Jacko switched on his laptop and projected a floor plan onto the whiteboard adjacent to the case details.

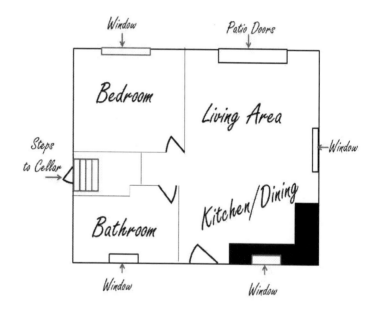

"I mocked up this plan on the computer after a conversation with Berriman Senior. Through the main entrance to the left is a bathroom and behind that a bedroom. The rest of this ground floor is open-plan with a kitchen/dining area at the front and a living space to the rear. There are four windows, two at the front and one at the rear in the bedroom and another between the kitchen and living areas on the right. The living area has patio doors to an outside grassed area and the path I described earlier. There's a door on the right of the building that gives access to the cellar below."

Jacko switched to the next slide.

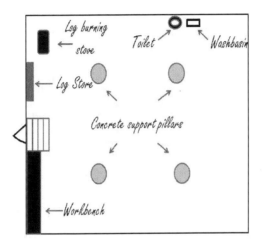

"Berriman could only tell me what was in the basement when the place was converted. He hasn't been in there since and apparently the son changed his job from a Paramedic to an Internet Trader shortly after he moved in and told his father he would be using it as nothing more than a storage facility. There are four concrete support pillars. A large workbench occupies the whole of the wall to the right of the steps. A log burning stove and wood storage box are to the left of the steps. On the back wall a toilet and wash basin were installed. There are no windows and only the side door gives access down into the basement. The internal access was sealed off during the conversion."

"Sounds like a fire officer's nightmare" said a voice from the audience.

"Probably" said Jacko, as he turned off the projector.

"Right, there are copies of these floor plans on the front

desk. Take one and familiarise yourselves with the layout of the building."

When Jacko had first shown Jake the plans and told him that the guy used to be a Paramedic he was convinced they had their man. He lived in the area in an isolated spot. The Berrimans spent time in their Portuguese villa every six months, leaving him alone there.

"Everything we've been told about this guy points to him being the abductor and the basement is an ideal holding place for the women he's abducted. So let's go and get this guy. No sirens, no fuss, we'll approach the place quietly and assess the situation. If he's there we don't want to panic him."

PART 2

34

Lagos Portugal, November 2009

"What was that all about?" Penny asked quizzically.

"I've just been speaking to a DC Jackson of the Thames Valley Police. Apparently my son is not all that he seems. Jackson told me they had located Harry in Melbourne, Australia and they were seeking confirmation of his identity from a Rob and Jenny Bishop. They were the house parents at the orphanage where Harry went when his mother had her breakdown".

"So who's the Harry that's living at Chapelgate?"

"Your guess is as good as mine, I just took him at face value. He had the family photo, same dark hair and blue eyes as Harry and knew everything there was to know about me and his mother. If he is an impostor he certainly fooled me."

"I've never said this before Harry, but I never really took to this so-called son of yours. Yes he was polite, said all the right things, in fact could be quite charming at times but I always felt uncomfortable in his presence. His eyes never quite reflected the words that came out of his mouth. To me they always held an air of hostility."

"Why didn't you say something before?"

"He was your son Harry and I know how pleased you were to have him back in your life."

"Even so love, had I known how you felt I wouldn't have suggested refurbishing the workshop so he could move in. I do know what you mean though, I often felt that we weren't as father and son should be although I put it down to the resentment he felt towards me for abandoning him when he was young. He was quite secretive, never really told me much about his life after the orphanage. I know he went off to Manchester, trained as a Paramedic and worked in the ambulance service there. He transferred to Newbury because he'd found out we were living in the area. Then after he moved in there he told me he was fed up with the job, didn't like his colleagues and that he was starting an internet based trading company. He didn't go into details about the business and any relationship we had was always on his terms. He didn't want me to visit without invitation so I only really saw him when he came to the house."

"Well I have to say I'm relieved he's not your Harry, but I think we should go back to England and find out just who is living on our property", said Penny.

Just as she said it the phone rang and Harry picked up. She could hear him describing the old workshop and basement in great detail and its position relative to the main house. He must be talking to the police again, Penny thought worriedly. Who was this guy and why were the police so interested in him and where he lived.

Harry put the phone down and looked at Penny.

"I think we have a real problem on our hands" he said. "It's been confirmed that Harry is in Melbourne so the police want to talk to this other guy urgently. They think he could be involved in some major investigation they're working on, wouldn't tell me what but wanted the layout of his living quarters, entrances and exits to the property, in fact almost a detailed plan of the estate. They are going over there to talk to him now apparently. I think you're right Pen, we should get home and see what the hell is going on."

With that he got on the phone to book them a flight back
to the UK.

35

Easter Sunday, 2007

He drove the 10-miles from Chapelgate to Didcot thinking about his so-called father Harry and his rich bitch Penny. How easy it had been for them to accept him into their lives. He lived rent free in a beautiful barn conversion in the midst of rural Berkshire, all courtesy of their generosity. Feeling guilty about neglecting him as a child was obviously the reason for his father's indulgence, however he could sense that she wasn't too happy about him living in such close proximity. Well tough titty lady I'm here to stay. They couldn't live forever and then, if he played his cards right, he would become a very wealthy man. If they lingered too long maybe he could just give them a nudge into the hereafter, until then he could scratch a living doing the rounds of the car boot sales buying cheap and selling on eBay. He arrived at the venue, it was Easter Sunday and the place was already filling up so he parked the car and began his search for bargains. Most of it was junk but every now and again he spotted a good prospect, negotiated a deal and by lunchtime had a reasonable haul of what he considered saleable items. Walking back to his car for the third time with a blue Maling lustre-ware vase from the 1950s tucked under his left arm and a bag full of Teenage Mutant Ninja Turtle toys in his right hand he was thinking £10 well spent should make me at least £50. With the stuff he'd already bought it was a good morning's work and would yield a healthy profit. Then he saw her, his mother was walking towards him looking just like she did in the photograph. The hairstyle was different, the clothes were different but the face was her face. A small blonde haired boy skipping beside her and clinging to her hand looked happy. For a split second he became that happy child enjoying the company of his mother on a day out, before the abuse began.

He almost panicked she was back. How could that happen? But it had and the evidence was right there in front of him. She can't be allowed to live, I'll have to kill her, no I want to kill her. Thank God she hadn't recognised him, she walked straight past without a second glance. For the next hour he followed them impatiently, watching her window shop and then stopping to buy the boy a boxed Dinky toy that he'd coveted from an earlier visit to that particular stall. At last she decided it was time to leave and made for the car park, he followed at a discreet distance and saw her stop beside a red hatchback Ford Ka with a 07 Oxfordshire registration. He almost ran to his car and was right behind her when she pulled out and headed northeast on Bowmont Water. He followed her for about ten miles, ending up on the A417 to Wantage where she turned left into a road called Hill Rise. A large pub with an equally large car park dominated the right hand corner of the road. Printed in large letters on a canvas sheet tied to the wooden fence surrounding the pub a slogan announced BOGOF on Main Meals 10am-6pm daily.

Harry smiled, until recently bog off had meant bugger off or get lost, now BOGOF was an acronym for buy one get one free. After a short distance the woman pulled into the driveway of a large 1950s/60s detached house. Harry stopped about 100-yards past the house, got out of the car, stretched and walked back towards it. Situated on the edge of town the location was perfect, allotments and open countryside nearby made the abduction he was already planning easy, not too many nosy neighbours. Later, as he drove out of Hill Rise, he smiled again wondering how the well-heeled residents liked being told to bog off every time they entered or left the road in which they lived.

On the drive home his head was filled with thoughts of his abusive mother. Seeing her again had brought back frightening memories of that abuse, making him nervous and afraid.

But he was a grownup now she couldn't hurt him anymore. This time he would be the one doing the hurting. Satisfied, and no longer afraid, his thoughts turned to retribution.

Other than putting a few things up for sale on eBay he spent the next two weeks finding out as much as he could about Jennifer Rawlings. That was the name his mother now called herself. She lived alone with her son on the eastern edge of Wantage, close to the Ridgeway. He knew the exact location, 12 Hill Rise, Wantage because he'd followed her there the first day he'd seen her and had checked it out several times since. With so much information available on-line he was able to find out her name, her marital status and the fact that her husband had been killed in Afghanistan in 2006. An article in the weekly rag at the time of his death had praised the local hero and given detailed information about his career and then went on to mention that she was a teacher at the local Primary School. Conveniently, the son was a pupil there too.

So the husband had gone, surprise, surprise, a familiar story, but luckily it meant no man around to complicate things. From observation he gathered she was content to fill her leisure hours at home with her son Simon. An elderly couple he assumed were her parents visited most weekends and that seemed to be her life, predictable.

Having worked as a Paramedic he formulated what he considered a fool-proof plan. Gaining access to the house and abducting his mother would be a breeze. Everyone trusted a Paramedic didn't they?

He drove Harry and Penny to Heathrow early on Saturday April 19th to catch their BA flight to Faro. He couldn't wait for them to leave.

As he drove back to Chapelgate he felt excited. Alone at last, and more than ready to punish his unsuspecting mother. But first things first, he'd go home and dig her grave.

36

Chapelgate, 2009

He'd woken Laura late last night, slamming the cellar door behind him and then flooding the space with artificial light.

She stared at him through bleary eyes and cursed.

"Please don't swear it's not becoming," he said grinning. "Sorry to wake you Mommie Dearest, just came to tell you tonight will be the last night you'll spend on that lumpy old mattress."

'Oh God,' thought Laura, this is it; this is where he rapes and kills me.'

"Don't worry it's not time to die just yet", he said, seeing her terrified expression. "I need to enjoy your company for a while longer. You saw the white gown in there?" He said as he pointed to the coffin. "Well tomorrow you will take off the clothes you are wearing and replace them with that. Make sure you do it Mommie Dearest or I will do it for you and think how undignified that would be. Then you will lie down in the coffin because that will be your new made to measure bed. Do I make myself clear?" he said menacingly.

"Why are you doing this?" Laura screamed. "What do you want from me? I thought at first it was about sex but it's not is it, it's about fear."

"Sex with you Mommie Dearest would be incest and that, as we know, is illegal. Anyway I'm not interested in sex. Why? Because you, Laura as you like to call yourself now, are responsible for creating me, the perfect misogynist. It's not even about fear, it's about exacting revenge for my childhood nightmares, but if you're afraid then that's an added bonus. Welcome to my world."

"You really are a madman. You think keeping me here against my will is legal?"

"Mad I'm not, angry I am" and with that he slapped her hard leaving the imprint of his hand on the left side of her face. "Show some respect."

"Respect has to be earned", she said angrily, clutching her face.

He hit her again, this time with such force she fell back to the mattress.

"Well you never earned mine either so shut your mouth unless you want more of the same."

Laura was crying, not through fear, she was no longer afraid, but now she too was angry.

"Hitting helpless women, very brave, very praiseworthy."

"Like hitting children I guess, they're kind of helpless too", he bent down and whispered the words through clenched teeth.

Laura changed tack.

"I've never had children and if I had I certainly wouldn't subject them to this."

"Lying bitch, that's right tell me it never happened, tell me I imagined it all."

"I'm not saying it didn't happen to you, what I'm saying is it wasn't me that did it."

"Oh but it was. I'm no fool, I recognize my own mother."

Laura, seeing there was no reasoning with him, shrugged.

"If that's what you believe so be it, but you're wrong."

"I've heard enough of your lies, just make sure you do what I told you" he said, as he climbed the steps, switched off the light and left her alone.

That was last night, this morning she had put on the white gown and was lying uncomfortably on her back in the coffin. She heard the cellar door open and sat up. He was carrying a breakfast tray and as he approached she noticed a camera hanging round his neck. 'Now what', she thought.

"Good, I see you've moved in. Right choice, we don't want any more unpleasantness."

"If you think lying on my back in this coffin wearing a shroud is something I find pleasurable then think again."

"Never happy are you?" he laughed.

He put down the tray on the floor beside the coffin and took the camera from round his neck.

"So now let's take your picture to add to my collection" he said, moving to the left hand wall and unveiling the photographs.

Standing aside he pointed to the A4 sized black and white prints. A woman dressed as she was and lying in a coffin was the subject of each and as she studied them she could see the fear in their eyes made more sinister by the monochrome photography.

Then, like a bolt from the blue she finally twigged what all this was about. He was the abductor - no he wasn't just an abductor he was a serial killer choosing his victims because they reminded him of his mother.

"Oh my God, I'm just the latest of many" she gasped.

"Number six" he smiled "and still they keep coming. Number seven is out there on the horizon."

Suddenly the look of fear in the other women's eyes was reflected in her own as he came toward her.

"Lie down" he snapped "perfect just perfect." He took the photograph and she knew he could see the fear too. Souvenirs of six helpless frightened women but then all serial killers wanted something to remember their victims by.

'I'll get this on the computer, get it printed, so you too can be added to my hall of fame. Believe me you will be famous soon." He replaced the cloth covering up the images once more.

Until now Laura had never been 100% sure that he would kill her, but kill her she knew he would. There would be no escape now, no rescue, her fate was undeniably sealed and she was scared not so much about dying but because of the way she knew she would die.
"How can you keep killing the same person over and over again?" she asked him.
"You tell me Mommie Dearest. How can you keep re-incarnating yourself over and over again? If you didn't there wouldn't be anyone to kill, now would there?"
"You believe in re-incarnation, poppycock, what you're doing is killing people that bear a resemblance to your mother. You're doing it because you enjoy doing it."
"Shut up you bitch."
"Not Mommie Dearest now then, just a bitch."
He looked at her with pure hatred.
"It won't work; you're trying to confuse me again. I'm sticking to my plan and my plan is to bury you alive and then to enjoy the thought of you desperately trying to breathe in the fast disappearing supply of air. Perfect retribution some would say."
"Only someone who's lost the plot completely" she said aggressively.

Ignoring her now he rolled up the mattress, tied it with string and stood it on end out of reach.
"Who knows, I might need it again if you do decide to come back. Who am I kidding; we both know you will be back."
"You'll make sure of that and will it even matter anymore whether or not they resemble your mother?"
"I really don't have time to listen to or be upset by the ravings of a desperate woman. Just eat your breakfast while it's still edible," he said pointing to the tray containing a

boiled egg, toast, marmalade and a mug of coffee.

Although she felt sick with fear Laura sat up and began to eat. Antagonising him further would probably earn her another beating and would achieve nothing. The food was almost cold and unappetising but she forced herself to eat it wondering if it would be her last meal.

He stood silently watching her as she ate.
"Right I'll leave you to it I have things to do", he said suddenly. "I'll be out for a couple of hours so try not to miss me too much."
"Drop dead" she murmured, unable to resist.
"Unlikely", he laughed, "I just hope you're in a better mood when I get back. In the meantime just think about your future, or lack of it."
"Go to hell."
"You'll be there first Mommie Dearest."

Mommie Dearest, I hate those words, Laura thought as he closed the door behind him.

37

Chapelgate

Jake and his team arrived at Chapelgate approximately 20-minutes after Harry had left. The gates were open so the two squad cars and the AVR drove straight in and parked outside the front door of the main house. Jake got out and signalled for the others to do the same. He could see that the space that should be occupied by the suspect's car was empty so chances were he was out. He stationed an armed officer and PC Johnson by the gate that led to the barn. He sent the other armed officers to check out the house which they did quickly and efficiently returning to report that it appeared to be empty.

"Okay, you two stay put" he said to the men at the gate "if he shows take him into custody, no unnecessary use of force but don't put yourselves at risk."
Jake turned and spoke to Sergeant Gordon.
"Get one of your men to get the enforcer from the AVR."
Gordon barked out the order, "you heard the DCI. Grimes go get it."
Grimes returned wearing protective gloves and carrying the specially designed manual battering ram.

Jake pulled the floor plan of the building from his pocket

and held it aloft.

"Ok you've all seen this layout; we need to make sure all the exits are covered. Coles take Talbot and cover the patio doors and rear windows. Hennessy, you and Sergeant Walsh cover the front of the property and Halliday watch the side window and call for assistance if you see anything. The rest of you come with me. Let's find out what's in this basement. Grimes you have the means get us inside."

As Jake suspected the door was locked so he signalled Grimes to use the ram. He made contact three times before the door yielded and burst open. A desperate scream filled the air and Jake, unable to see into the dark space below, immediately shouted. "Don't move, armed police officers."

He fumbled around the wall inside the door, found the light switch and flicked it on. His eyes scanned the basement, he didn't see any movement.
"I'll go in first Sir" offered Sergeant Gordon who was armed with a Taser stun gun. Grimes put down the enforcer on the top step, drew his own Taser and followed him down. Seconds later Gordon called up.
"Basement's secured Sir, no threat here."

Jake, Mo and the rest of the team poured down the steps amazed to see a woman sitting up in the midst of a white coffin clinging tightly to Grimes. Jake walked over, looked down at her tear stained face and simply asked "Laura Marks?"

Mo was horrified; the monster was actually keeping the woman in a coffin in his cellar. As she got closer she could see the chain around Laura's ankle that shackled her to one of the support pillars, giving her a small measure of movement to use the facilities if she needed to. She also appeared to be dressed in some sort of burial gown.

Jake introduced himself.

"Yes" said Laura, "he told me you were in charge of the search. You know he's insane, he thinks I'm his mother. Apparently she used to lock him in the cellar or in the coal box when he was a child. He gets his sick, so-called revenge by burying his victims alive, keeping them alive underground by pumping air into the coffin and then he just decides to cut the supply and let them die a slow and horrible death." Scarcely drawing breath between sentences the words just spewed out from her mouth. 'Probably from pure relief,' Jake thought.

Mo held out her hand.
"Let's get you out of there" she said, and turned to Gregg.
"Dave, see if there's anything over that bench to cut her free and then we'll organize an ambulance to take you off to hospital for a check over."
"Not an ambulance" shouted Laura "he's a Paramedic so please I don't want one anywhere near me. Call it irrational but that's how I feel."
"Okay, okay" said Mo, gently stroking Laura's hair "we'll get a squad car to take you there."
"He fractured my nose, told me how to treat it so it feels almost normal now."
"Looks fine" said Mo "however, I'm sure the doctors will give you a thorough check over. Did he assault you in any other way?"
"He hit me a couple of times when I called him crazy. Didn't sexually assault me thank God but then I am his mother supposedly and as he said that would be incest. Said he hated women and it was all about revenge."

Spunky woman thought Mo as she turned to Jake and raised her eyebrows quizzically as if to say this all points to a connection to Harry Berriman. He'd stood back thinking it was better that a woman should deal with Laura in her frightened and vulnerable state. But he was just as perplexed as Mo.

Dave Gregg freed Laura from her ankle restraint with bolt

cutters he'd found inside the workbench.

"There love, you're free at last, no need to worry about that Roland anymore."

Laura looked at him curiously.

"Sorry love, roll and butter, nutter."

"He's a cockney" said Mo, apologetically.

"Thank you Gregg" said Jake, impatiently. "Halliday take a squad car and get Ms Marks to casualty ASAP. Mo you go along too and Laura just one thing before you go, do you know where he is?"

"Just said he was going out for a while, didn't say where or why."

"Ok thanks. We'll take your statement later, when you're feeling less fragile."

Mo took Laura's arm and they followed Halliday out of the cellar.

"Gregg go up and get the others down here now" said Jake.

After a couple of minutes everyone was gathered in the basement listening to Jake's plan.

"Okay, looks as if he'll be back here shortly. Sgt Gordon, Grimes and Miller will stay put here with me. We want everything to look normal here so the rest of you take all the vehicles and park up in the village as inconspicuously as possible. I'll call you if and when we need you. Meanwhile we'll stay hidden here and hopefully apprehend him without anyone getting hurt."

"Sounds like a plan Sir' said Walsh "right men let's go."

Jake heard the cars pull off the driveway.

"Miller, you and Grimes cover the access through the hedge, Sgt Gordon and I will cover the gate near his parking spot. Stay out of sight ok?"

They all nodded their agreement made their way out of the basement and took up their positions.

As Harry approached Chapelgate he saw three police cars exit right onto the main road towards East Ilsley. 'God they've found me' he thought 'don't panic Harry they haven't found you, they've just found Chapelgate. Summers is a smart bastard, he must have left cops on the estate ready to nab me, in fact I bet he's there too. Well fuck you Jake, bad timing, I've seen you,' he smiled gleefully and followed the cars into the village where they turned right by the duck pond.

"Bye plods" he said, putting up two fingers in a V sign as he drove straight on through Compton to the A34 and into Newbury.

Thirty minutes later wearing a cap and scarf by way of a partial disguise he booked into a Premier Inn about five miles from Newbury for three nights. He signed in as Henry Baxter, handed over the credit card from the account he had set up in that name, collected the key and took up residence in room 34. Throwing himself on the bed he smiled at his good fortune. He'd seen the cops before they saw him, the room here had been available, and he didn't need to pass reception again until checking out time so everything was just fine.

After four hours of hanging round Chapelgate Jake knew they'd been rumbled and called it a day. He phoned the station and organised for scenes of crime officers to attend and about thirty minutes later Mike Long and his team arrived.

"We've finally found the bastards lair Mike but he's avoided capture. See what you can find. We're looking for bodies as well as evidence. The five missing women could well be buried here."

"I'm bringing in dogs to search the site, if there are human remains they'll sniff 'em out" Mike said, confidently.

"I'll stand my men down now and we'll head back to Newbury. Keep me informed."

Jake and his team drove back to Newbury in silence, each one feeling tired and cheated. Mo was in the office when he arrived back.

"How's Laura?"

"She'll be fine, her nose is healing well and she doesn't have any other physical injuries. They'll keep her in overnight for observation and she's seeing a psychologist tomorrow, after that she'll probably be allowed home. She seems very strong mentally Guv, yes it's been an ordeal for her but I think with care and counselling she'll mend quickly without much lasting trauma. I guess we can get a statement from her after the assessment tomorrow. I phoned Dan Williams, told him the good news and he arrived at the hospital before I left and Laura certainly felt well enough to give him earache."

"Good. Not so good is the fact we've lost this guy, he must have seen activity at the house and scarpered."

"We'll get him Guv, at least he knows we're onto him."

"I really hope so. Come into my office there's something I need to show you."

Mo followed him into his office closing the door behind her.

"You're being mysterious Jake" she reverted to his Christian name now they were alone and out of earshot of the others.

Jake turned on his PC and called up the profile that Jaime had sent.

"Come and look at this", he said.

She leaned over his shoulder and read the document.

"From what we know it seems fairly accurate. Who wrote it?"

"Jaime did. We met up the night you and Jess went to the Watermill."

"You sly fox, Jake Summers, you both kept very quiet about that. You told me not to discuss the case in front of her the night you came to dinner, remember?"

"I didn't know her background then. The fact that she'd been a student of Gus Harrison put her in the category 'very useful to have on board' and I thought why not make use of her talents."

"And knowing that gave you an excuse to get cosy with my sister-in-law," she laughed.

"No such thing", Jake said, and actually blushed. "I really thought she could help, it was purely professional. Ask her if you don't believe me."

"Oh be sure I will." She winked at him and left.

Now came the hard bit, he had to phone Helen Davis and tell her the suspect was not in custody.

38

Royal Berkshire Hospital

Less than 24-hours since she was admitted Laura was already fed up with being in hospital, doctors checking her physically and mentally, there was nothing wrong with her she just wanted to go home and get back to some sort of normality. Dan arrived yesterday afternoon full of tearful apologies and promises, saying it was his fault she'd been abducted, how he should never have left her alone and never would again if she gave him another chance. How all this had brought him to his senses and made him realise just how much she meant to him and how devastated he would be if he'd lost her. After an hour of pleading she finally gave in.

"Ok one more chance but if you blow it this time that's it, we're done."

"Oh believe me I won't", said one very relieved man.

She'd sent him away then telling him she wanted to rest and told him to come back tomorrow with clean clothes for her to go home in. Sgt Connolly had left some time ago but there was still a young uniformed officer stationed outside her hospital room. Feeling warm and safe she drifted off to sleep quite quickly.

This morning Dan was back waiting impatiently for them to finish the tests. Sgt Connolly and DCI Summers were here and asking to interview her. The doctors were happy for them to do so. Here they all were, Dan sitting by her bed clasping her hand and the two detectives standing on the other side. Sgt Connolly stood with a poised pen and open notebook ready for action.

Jake spoke first.

"Laura, first let me say we are so pleased you're free and relatively unharmed. We will do all in our power to catch the guy responsible. In the meantime take your time and describe what happened on the day you were abducted."

She told them how she'd woken up feeling really angry with Dan for staying out all night and how that anger had translated into the blinds being pulled down and the clothes being stashed in the holdall. Jake was pleased to see that Dan was looking suitably sheepish. She went on to tell them how he'd gained access to the flat, pretending to be a Paramedic and then subsequently how she'd woken up in the basement as his captive having no idea of where she was or how she'd got there.

Jake listened intently while Mo scribbled in her notebook.

"Must have been a terrifying experience for you" Jake said sympathetically.

"At first yes but then I just got mad. I almost escaped you know, but he had hidden camera's installed in the basement so was watching me the whole time."

Jake was impressed by her spirit and said as much.

"Now the really important thing Laura, we need a description of this man."

"That's easy" she said, "I'll remember him for the rest of my life. White male, probably about my age, between 5ft 11ins and 6ft 1in tall, dark brown hair which he wears brushed forward into a sort of fringe, could be covering up a receding hairline, blue piercing eyes, clean shaven, oval shaped face, aquiline nose, white even teeth, and slim but muscular build. Not bad looking really for a murderer and mad man. Oh and he spoke with a local accent so I guess that means he was brought up in the area."

"Wow, that description could have been given by a seasoned police officer" said Mo.

"Avid crime novel reader", replied Laura. "The other thing, he showed me a photograph of his family when he was a youngster and I have to say I do bear an uncanny likeness to his mother."

Jake turned to look at Mo who raised her eyebrows.

"Just like it's not you in that photo, it's not him either", she said.

"What do you mean not him?" Laura looked perplexed.

"That photograph went missing a long time ago and the boy in it now lives with his family in Australia."

"So why does my captor think she's his mother?" Laura asked, looking completely baffled.

"I have an idea" said Jake. "Thanks Laura, we may need to speak to you again soon, until then stay safe."

As he and Mo started to leave the room the doctor arrived and told Laura she could go home.

"Hang on a minute, you can't run out like that with no explanation" she called out accusingly.

"You'll be the first to know if it pans out, but I won't give false hope of an early arrest on a snippet of an idea."

"Make sure you take care of our star witness", he said as he turned to Dan. "There'll be a squad car parked outside your flat at all times until we have this guy in custody and don't forget, Sgt Connolly and I are just a phone call away ok?"

"I'll take care of her for sure but it's good to know we have police protection too."

39

After leaving the flat, and as soon as they were in the car, Mo began to quiz him.

"So what is this idea Guv?"

"Well if Berriman lost the photo when he was a resident at Stirling House, the chances are someone from there took it, and who shared his room and was his so called best mate?"

"Of course, Johnny Price", she responded.

"The very same. Right, ring Rob Bishop and tell him we're on our way over and let's see if we get an ID from the description Laura gave us."

Minutes later they were on their way.

"Slow down Mo we don't want to be stopped for speeding and besides, I'd like to arrive in one piece" Jake laughed, as the speedometer hit eighty five.

"No worries, I'm just anxious to verify your theory."

"No more than me. Taking five more minutes won't change the outcome."

"Ok Guv, point taken." The speedometer dropped back to sixty.

As they arrived Rob Bishop came to the door and beckoned them in.

"Your phone call sounded urgent Sergeant" he said, smiling at Mo.

Before Mo could answer Jake butted in.

"We've found the latest abductee alive and well. Unfortunately the offender eluded capture. However, Laura Marks was able to give us a detailed description of him. According to Laura he had the Berriman family photograph. We know that Harry either lost it or had it stolen from him, so we were wondering if the abductor could be one of the other boys' resident here at that time."

Rob ushered them into the sitting room where Jenny was waiting.

"Good news Jen, they've found the missing woman Laura Marks and she's ok."

"Thank God, well done you" said Jenny Bishop, beaming at the two detectives.

"Thank you Mrs Bishop" said Jake, smiling. "Perhaps you can identify someone from the description that Laura gave us of the man that abducted her."

"Why would I be able to do that?" Jenny asked, looking puzzled.

"They think one of the other boys may have stolen Harry's family photo", Rob interrupted before Jake could answer.

"That's right Mr Bishop."

"So let's hear it then", said Jenny, impatiently.

Mo opened her notebook and read out Laura's description of her abductor.

"I haven't seen him since he went to Manchester but it sounds a lot like Johnny Price", exclaimed Jenny, "except it can't be him, he had brown eyes."

"Yes definitely brown eyes", Rob nodded his agreement.

"Could the witness have made a mistake about the eye colour?"

"I doubt it, she was pretty specific" said Jake, letting his disappointment show. "What about the other boys, any of them fit the description?"

"Not really, most of them were older, the only other boy with dark hair and blue eyes was Jimmy Keegan aged 15 at the time, he spoke with a strong Irish brogue, lovely lad.

Charm the birds from the trees that one" replied Jenny, with obvious fondness.

"Well thanks for your help, we'd better get back to the station or they'll think we've deserted."

"Before you go, thanks for sending Harry's letter back and for the photo he sent. I told you it wouldn't be him didn't I?" said Jenny.

"You did Mrs Bishop, you obviously know your boys well" Jake said reluctantly, and he felt like a naughty schoolboy being chastised for criticising one of hers.

It started to rain quite heavily as they left.

"Bloody weather" said Mo, as she ran and jumped into the driver's seat.

"Back to the station then Guv?" asked Mo, driving away. Jake noticed the Bishops framed in the doorway of Stirling House and raised his hand in farewell and thought 'good honest caring people.'

"No let's go to Salter Street, Laura should be home now and we can ask her about the guy's eye colour."

"She sounded pretty sure to me" countered Mo "but it's worth a try."

Jake broke the silence.

"I'd like to come round tonight and bounce some ideas off you and Jaime. She provided a pretty accurate profile and I'd like to know what you both think about the Isabelle Berriman connection, the photograph and a few other issues that we can't quite fathom yet. Ok?"

"Ok by me, does Jaime know?"

"No, I'll ring when we get back."

The only sound for the rest of the journey was the hypnotic swish of the wiper blades against the windscreen allowing them moderate visibility through the pounding rain.

"God we're here already", Jake sounded surprised, as they pulled up outside the flats in Salter Street.

"Want me with you Guv or shall I stay in the car?"

"Worried about getting your hair wet Mo?" he asked, amused.

"You've tumbled me Guv."

"Get out of the car Connolly" he said, good naturedly "we'll do this together."

"Slave driver" she said, jumping out quickly and running inside the front door of the flats before he'd even moved.

Williams answered the door and looked surprised to see them again so soon.

"Back already, did your idea work out?"

"Not too sure yet, I just need to check something with Laura if that's ok?"

"You'd better come in then" he sounded annoyed "she was just about to lie down."

"We won't stay long' Jake said, apologetically as he and Mo followed Dan inside.

Laura had heard their voices and looked at them expectantly as they joined her in the sitting room.

"You have news already?" She said eagerly.

"Sorry to disappoint but we're just here to verify part of the description you gave us. If the abductor had brown eyes we may have a positive ID. Is there any possibility that you could be mistaken about his eye colour?" Jake asked hopefully.

"That's it" Laura blurted out "the second time I saw him there was something different about him that I couldn't quite put my finger on at the time. But that's it, he had brown eyes. Every other time I saw him they were blue."

Mo looked at Jake excitedly.

"Coloured contact lenses; he was wearing coloured contact lenses."

"Does that mean you know who he is?" Laura demanded after hearing the excitement in Mo's voice.

"I can only say we know who it could be" said Jake, evasively.

"So do I get to know?" Laura asked, sounding indignant.

"Regretfully no, we can't release that information at present, anyway it may prove to be a wild goose chase, and the fellow could be completely innocent. You'll know as soon as we've made an arrest and you're called in to identify him. Until then thanks again for your help."

Laura looked annoyed and Jake sympathised, but rules were rules and he wasn't about to break any and jeopardise this case, it was too important. And if the press got hold of it all hell would break loose.

Outside again they noticed that a squad car had arrived and was parked nearby. Jake walked over, recognised Halliday and Talbot, signalled for them to wind down the window and stuck his head into the car.

"Keep your eyes open and keep her safe lads. She's the only one who can positively ID this bastard when we catch him."

"Depend on it Sir" said Halliday earnestly.

40

Newbury Police Station

Jake, Mo and DCs Gregg, Miller and Jackson were crammed into Jake's office reviewing the case when Helen Davis arrived.

"We need to talk", she said to Jake as she opened the door.

The others respectfully left and Helen sat down opposite Jake.

"I see you've circulated the suspect's description in an All Ports Warning so hopefully that will prevent him from leaving the country."

"Not guaranteed but a sensible precaution we felt Mam."

"I also got your message about this fellow Johnny Price, you think he's our abductor?" she asked.

"Could be Mam, he shared a room at Stirling House with Harry Berriman. The Bishops' mentioned him immediately when Laura's description was read out to them. Now we think he wore coloured contact lenses to pass himself off as Berriman junior. We have no idea why he would take Berriman's name, abduct and possibly kill look-alikes of Harry's mother Isabelle. It makes no sense whatsoever. I would like to show you something Mam." He opened his desk drawer withdrew Jaime's 'offender profile' and passed it across to Helen Davis.

"Interesting" she said, and handed it back to Jake. "When and who" she said, pointedly.

"A couple of days ago by a friend, Jaime Mason, former colleague of Gus Harrison" Jake explained.

"I'm impressed, it's good. Gus Harrison's protégé eh? Well, she was certainly trained by the best."

"I was impressed too and I'd like to see if she has any theories as to why this offender would commit crimes in another's name and for abuse that he himself didn't actually suffer."

"I trust that this woman is discreet and trustworthy?" Helen said, raising an inquiring eyebrow.

"Absolutely, I guarantee it one hundred per cent Mam, no question about it."

"Ok, let's see if she can shed any light."

"Thank you Mam, I'll get back to you if she does. Oh, and Inspector Long and his forensic team are busy at Chapelgate. They're using dogs to search for any human remains on site. Laura Marks said he admitted to killing the other five women by burying them alive and heaven forbid if we hadn't arrived in time she would've suffered the same fate."

"Gruesome." Helen Davis wrinkled her nose in disgust as she said it. "Get Ms Marks to do a photo fit and get it on TV and in the papers ASAP, don't give this guy anywhere to hide."

"Already in hand, Mam. Sergeant Connolly is taking Bob Jessop to see Laura first thing tomorrow. He's the best so the press will have it by the afternoon."

"Ok Jake, call me if Long and his team find any bodies. At least then the relatives will get a sort of closure."

Helen Davis rose to leave and turned to Jake with a smile.

"Jaime Mason a close friend Jake?"

"Early days, Mam." Jake felt his face flush.

As she left the office Jake picked up the phone and called Jaime.

"I know they're out" Jake whispered, as she picked up the

phone. "It's me, your partner in crime."

"DCI Summers I presume," she said laughing "I hadn't realised we were partners in anything. What can I do for you?"

"Plenty" he chuckled "seriously, have you spoken to Mo today?"

"Not yet, I was switched to answer phone until a few minutes ago. I've been writing all day."

"Laura Marks has given us a good description of her abductor", he said.

"So?"

"Well, we think it could be a Johnny Price, someone Harry Berriman roomed with at the orphanage. To cut to the chase, can Mo and I pick your brains tonight? We're at a loss to understand why he would commit these crimes?"

"Ok, but I'll need a complete rundown of the boy's life. Why he was in the boy's home, what his background was, everything that could have moulded his personal development."

"I'm onto it already. See you later."

He put the phone down and headed out of his office. He stopped at Mo's desk.

"Get on the blower to the Bishops and find out all there is to know about Price. Jaime needs it for our meeting tonight."

"You've phoned her then" she smirked.

"No, I sent smoke signals. Of course I phoned her" he sounded annoyed.

"Sorry-eee , just asking".

"No I'm sorry Mo" he apologised "I just want this case put to bed."

"We all do Guv but we're getting there now. Come and eat with us tonight, we'll get Chinese and you can foot the bill."

"Done and thanks, I'd love to and again sorry for my bad temper."

"Goes with the territory, it's tough at the top."

"Tell me about it" he said smiling.

As he returned to his desk the phone rang, it was Mike Long.

"You need to get back here Sir", Mike sounded despondent "we're pretty sure we've found the bodies, all five of them, buried in shallow graves between the barn conversion and a small copse at the perimeter boundary, about fifty yards from the cellar door. There's one freshly dug and unoccupied, probably ready to house the body of Laura Marks. The sick bastard's marked each grave with a cypress tree. I know that particular tree well and it's often associated with death or with the passage into the afterlife for eternity."

"You're a mine of information on the macabre Mike" Jake quipped.

"You learn all sorts in this job. Anyway we've recovered one body from the first grave and we've erected a speed tent over it. I've called in Freddie Saunders so we'll hang fire here until Saunders arrives and then dig them up one at a time."

"On my way Mike."

Jake slammed the phone down, grabbed his coat and headed for the door. Seeing Mo was on the phone and scribbling furiously he signalled for her to hold.

"That was Mike Long, they've found bodies at Chapelgate. I'll take Miller and get over there now; you and Gregg follow on as soon as soon as you've finished with the Bishops."

"Closure" said Mo sadly, and went back to her conversation with Rob Bishop.

41

Chapelgate

As Jake pulled off the main road he could see a few members of the public peering in through the driveway gates. Mike Long had closed them and stationed one of his officers there to prevent nosey sightseers invading the site. Jake blew his horn and leaned out of the driver's window.

"There's nothing to see here, why don't you all just go on home?"

"Really mate", said a ruddy faced man with an enormous beer belly, "rumour has it that this is the abductor's lair."

"Yeah, we heard it in the Swan last night," said an equally fat woman. "So we thought we'd come down and take a look, didn't we Cliff?" she said to beer belly.

"Nice day for a family outing" Jake said sarcastically as he spotted the young boy pushed against the gate in front of them.

Jake got out, flashed his warrant card at the young police officer who immediately opened the gates allowing him to drive in. The driveway was littered with police vehicles so Jake parked in front of the side gate that led to the barn conversion and its basement. White suited forensic officers were everywhere. As Jake approached the white police tent he recognised the sharp featured, balding and bespectacled personage of Freddie Saunders. The stocky forensic pathologist was inside bending down awkwardly and inspecting the contents of an open coffin.

"Freddie" said Jake.
"Good to see you Jake." Freddie straightened and shook the extended hand.
"What've we got?"
"Almost certainly a female body, advanced decomposition therefore must have been in the ground for a couple of years or more. Probably his first victim."
"Jennifer Rawlings", said Jake.
"Take a look at that" said Saunders, pointing to the coffin lid at the back of the tent.

An acrylic pipe about 3ft long protruded above the surface of the lid. Some sort of bung had been pushed down into it and the tube was filled with earth.
"He was about to bury Laura Marks in an identical coffin, said the pipe allowed him to pump in air" explained Jake.
"Until he cruelly sealed it and cut off the supply. Now take a look at the underside of the lid", said Freddie.

Jake turned it over and was horrified to see clearly defined scratch marks covered with what appeared to be dried blood.
"A fruitless attempt to escape before she asphyxiated", Freddie suggested.

Jake turned to Miller who looked pale and angry.
"Phone the station Dusty, tell Sergeant Connolly and Gregg to stay put, they can't do anything here."
"For her we're two years too late" Miller muttered.
"You'll be taking the remains back to the lab with you Freddie?" asked Jake.
"We will, as soon as we've disinterred them all. We expect to see varying levels of decomposition depending on the time spent underground. The body buried six months ago should be more intact and probably easier to identify, but

you know this will take time Jake. There's a lot to deal with, I may need some outside help."

"Well I'll let you get on with it. Mike a word before we go."

Jake walked away from the coffin, Mike alongside him and Dusty behind them.

"Find anything inside?" asked Jake.

"Plenty, he may be insane but he's a clever bastard. He installed cameras in the basement to monitor his victims' movements. I'll hand his PC over to our computer buffs and see what they can recover. He may have kept footage or records of the other victims. The most damning evidence is a set of photographs hanging on the wall of the basement. He actually photographed his victims in their coffins before he buried them alive. There are framed, monochrome, photographs of all five. They all look absolutely terrified. Evil bastard probably taunted Laura with them. He keeps a supply of empty frames and photographic paper in his apartment probably for future use. We've taken his camera and will be looking at the images on his memory card. We'll probably find one of Laura there or on his PC. We've lifted several sets of prints from the basement and will be checking them against the ones we have on file and hopefully we'll get positive IDs from those too. We found a few blonde hairs lying around and there's evidence of Laura everywhere. The comb, the toothbrush everything she touched or used we'll be bagging and taking back to the lab. Oh and we found a sheet of that adhesive he used to convert the car windows to mirrored glass. And guess what? We found a shed full of power tools, sheets of MDF board and a paper pattern. In fact everything he would need to make the perfect coffin. This guy's a man of many talents. "

"All used for the wrong reasons. Well done Mike. It seems you've unearthed an Aladdin's cave. Keep me informed of any other developments", said Jake.

"You off now?"

"Not much point hanging around just watching you and

your merry men dig up more bodies."

Dusty Miller slid into the driver's seat.
"Back to the station then Guv?" he asked Jake.
"Yeah, but go the back way via Farnborough and then on to the B4494, it's quieter and probably quicker at this time of day. The A34 will be chaotic with the road works near Chieveley."

Going through the gates Jake noticed that beer belly and family were still there.
"Like vultures waiting for carrion to appear" he commented contemptuously.
"Vultures indeed Guv, feeding off the misery of others", was Miller's reply.
"Did you see what she was doing Guv?" Jake shook his head. "She was actually standing there knitting."
"Expecting the guillotine to appear and heads to roll then? Unbelievable."

He also noticed that the press had arrived in numbers. Cameras poised hoping, as always, to cash in on the misfortune of others. The major nationals were there and he recognised Jim Raymond, a reporter with the local paper. Jim had written a series of sympathetic articles about the women and their relatives and was genuinely interested in finding out the unembellished truth about their abductions and the effect it had on their loved ones. Jake had a real regard for the man and his work and he was surprised that one of the nationals hadn't snapped him up. On reflection, they'd probably tried but Jim wouldn't compromise his integrity and reputation as a journalist by resorting to 'a story at any cost' mentality. Jim saw him and raised his hand in greeting; the rest crowded around the car and shouted questions through the closed window. He wound it down slowly and immediately microphones were thrust into the car and the cacophony of sound almost deafened him.
"Back off" he shouted angrily "there'll be a press

conference at Newbury Police Station at 2:30pm this afternoon. I'll give you a statement then and any questions you have will be addressed there. Until then just let us get on with the job."

Temporarily satisfied they did back off allowing him to close the window and Miller to drive away.
"Meanwhile back in the real world, when we get back Dusty get down to Oxford Road and see if Archie Jenkins recognises the guy from the description Laura gave us. I'll catch up with Sergeant Connolly and see what she gleaned from the Bishops."

It had been a shit day but the sun was shining and Jake felt his mood lighten as he leaned back against the passenger head rest. A few brown and yellow lifeless leaves still clung to the skeletal branches that arched from trees on either side of the narrow road forming a tunnel through which they drove. Nature had a way of transforming the most dismal of days.

Day-dreaming and enjoying the journey along this quiet country back road Jake was, without warning, thrown forward against his seat belt when Miller slammed on the brakes.
"What the hell", he shouted, suddenly alert.
"Sorry Sir", Miller interrupted, "a deer ran out in front of me."
As he said it six more Fallow Deer crossed the road in front of their vehicle and disappeared into the hedgerow.
"Christ Dusty, I was miles away you scared the shit out of me."
"I scared myself. What can I say Guv. Deer are one of the hazards you're likely to encounter driving these back roads."
"Ok Dusty, I know I told you to come this way, you've made your point" Jake laughed, "just try and get me back to the station in one piece."

42

Miller dropped Jake off outside the station.

"Right Guv, I'll catch up with Archie Jenkins. See if he knows our suspect. Report in later."

Jake waved him off, walked inside and seeing Mo he immediately beckoned her into his office. Knowing exactly why, Mo picked up her notebook and followed him in.

"No Dusty? Did you leave him at Chapelgate?" she asked.

"No, I sent him to see Jenkins. See if he recognises the description of Price. What'd you get from the Bishops?"

"Not much really", she replied. "I spoke to Rob first and he said they knew nothing at all about the boy's background. He was a foundling whose parents were never identified. He was sent to Stirling House from some sort of nursery/orphanage when he was five-years-old and stayed there until he was sixteen. Apparently he was quite a bright lad and keen to get away from Stirling House and the stigma of being brought up in a boys' home. The local authority found him lodgings and he started to train as a draughtsman. He stuck at it for six months and then moved to Manchester. That was the last time the Bishops heard anything about him. He's never been in touch.

I spoke to Jenny next and she was a bit more informative. She said Johnny really resented the fact that he had no family. Most of the other kids had relatives that visited from time to time, he had no one. She described him as a loner who didn't mix well so initially she was pleasantly surprised when he befriended Harry. But then she said he only did that on his terms. If Harry didn't do exactly as he said then Johnny would either punch him or refuse to speak to him for days. And, as Jenny said, that became very awkward when they were sharing a room. She recalled an incident when Price decided that he and Harry should become blood brothers and then cut Harry's hand so badly that he had to have stitches. In fact, after that incident Harry was moved to another room and had little more to do with Price. Afterwards Price became more aggressive and was always taunting Harry about his mad mother. Jenny made it perfectly clear without actually spelling it out that she didn't really care for Johnny Price. She described him as an emotionless bully who didn't give a damn about anything or anyone and very difficult to like."

"Jenny Bishop said that!" Jake was astonished. "You do surprise me. I can't imagine her disliking anyone, especially one of her boys."

"Well she did and still does. I think she's twigged that Price could be the abductor and before I hung up she said quote 'I told Rob years ago that genes will out'. So we didn't get much from them, but probably enough to take to Jaime tonight and see what she makes of it."

"I'll be over about 7:30pm. I'll have to go home first and feed Hobbs or I'll suffer his withering looks and loud complaints."

"I told you, I just love that cat." Mo said as she left his office laughing.

43

Stirling House, 1991

Harry was upset he couldn't find his photograph. He was sure he'd put it in the drawer of his bedside cabinet inside *The Gremlins* by Roald Dahl, the book he was in the middle of reading. He'd shaken the book, leafed through it several times, no photograph. A strange thought crossed his mind; perhaps the mischievous gremlins had hidden it. "Don't be so stupid", he said out loud.

"Why are you being stupid?" Johnny Price asked, walking into the room behind him.
"I'm not" said Harry, feeling embarrassed that someone had heard him. "I'm upset because I've lost the photo of my mum and dad. It's all I had left of my family" and he started to cry.

Johnny came over put his hand on Harry's shoulder.
"I've got a great idea", he said excitedly. "Let's be blood brothers then I can be your family. It's easy I've read about it, all we have to do is make a small cut on our hands and mix our blood together."

With that he smashed his bedside lamp picked up a jagged piece of glass and moved towards Harry.

"I'm not sure" Harry said, looking warily at the advancing boy. "I bet it will hurt."

"Don't be such a wuss" said Johnny, drawing the glass slowly across his right hand and watching the blood trickle out. "See it hardly hurt at all, hold out your hand." Harry did and Johnny cruelly dug the glass shard into his hand.

"That really hurt" said Harry, snatching his hand away.

"Stop whinging" said Johnny, pulling at Harry's bleeding hand. "Put it on mine before the blood dries, that's it, now we're blood brothers for life."

Harry's hand was badly cut and very painful.

"I'm going to find Mother Jenny and see if she can stop it bleeding" he said.

"Don't tell her what we've done, just say you knocked the lamp off by accident and cut yourself picking up the pieces."

Harry ran downstairs and found Jenny in the kitchen.

"I've cut my hand" he said, holding it out towards her.

"That looks really nasty", she said, taking his hand, "how on earth did it happen? How did you cut it so badly?"

He repeated Johnny's fib.

"You'll need some stitches in it; I'll get Rob to run you to the surgery. Just picking up broken glass you say. It looks very deep, are you sure that's what happened?"

"Yes that's what happened."

Upstairs Johnny Price was smiling as he took Harry's photo from his jacket pocket.

"Hello mum, hello dad, I'm Harry now. Never had a proper mum and dad before never knew who they were till now. You treated me so badly mum, why did you do that? Why did you let them bring me here?"

An hour later Rob arrived back with a sheepish Harry in tow. The doctor who stitched his hand was unconvinced by the boy's explanation of how the injury happened and told Rob as much. On the way home after some questioning Harry admitted the truth.

"Ok, let's go and find your mate Johnny shall we?" Rob said, as they came into the hall.

Upstairs they found him kicking a football against his bedroom door.
"Up to more mischief Johnny? How often have you been told about kicking a ball inside the house?"
He looked up at Rob with a defiant grin.
"You can wipe that smile off your face right now. Harry here has just had his hand stitched, know anything about his injury?"
"No, why would I?" He said sullenly.
"Show me your hands Johnny." He held them out and Rob noticed the small cut across the palm of the boy's right hand.
"Get that picking up broken glass too did you? You could have done irreparable damage to Harry's hand cutting it as deeply as you did. Fortunately for you he only needed a few stitches. Blood brothers indeed, you can both stay in your room for the rest of the day." With that he opened their bedroom door ushered them in, closed it firmly behind them and went downstairs.

"Sneak" said Johnny, punching Harry on the arm.
"I don't want to be your blood brother" Harry complained.
"Too late bruv, you are."

Downstairs Rob gave Jenny a run-down of what had happened. She was furious.
"That Johnny Price has the devil in him; he barely scratched his own hand you say but nearly maimed Harry and then told him to lie about it. Do you think we should inform Social Services?" Informing Social Services was Jenny's answer to everything.
"No, but I do think we should log the incident in his report book and keep more of an eye on him in future, now we know what he's capable of."
"We know nothing of that boy's background. The nursery named him after that PC Price, the bobby that found him.

The mother that abandoned him as baby was never identified. For all we know he could be the son of some criminal type and a street walker."

"Calm down love", Rob laughed, "your imagination's running riot. He could equally be the son of a young couple who weren't old enough to cope with the responsibility of a baby." Rob put his arm round Jenny, "I know why I love you Mrs Bishop, you make me laugh'."

"Time will tell, genes will out", she said as she shrugged him off.

44

Croft Cottage, Hermitage

Jake arrived at Croft Cottage at 7:20pm.

"Hobbs let you leave early then, come in." Mo led the way through to the sitting room where Jess and Jaime were deep in conversation. They both looked up briefly as Jake walked in, said hello and carried on talking about the plot of Jaime's current novel. He sat down winked at Mo and waited. Five minutes later Jaime looked at him. "Sorry Jake, just something I wanted to run by my literary critic here. How are you?"

"Fine thank you my lady" he quipped. Mo and Jess exchanged quizzical looks.

"My Lady, what's all that about?" Mo asked.

"Just our little joke" he said, smiling at Jaime.

"That's it?" Mo inquired after several moments of silence, "you're not going to enlighten us further?"

"Don't think so" said Jake, shrugging his shoulders.

"Jaime?" Jess appealed to her sister.

"You heard the man, don't think so."

"Please yourself" Jess said, feigning annoyance "just don't ask for free critical advice again."

"Oooh! Get over yourself will you Sis", and they all laughed.

"I'll get it" said Jake, springing to his feet as the doorbell rang.

He opened the door to a smiling Chinese lad wearing a crash helmet and carrying two paper sacks advertising Kim Lee's Chinese Takeaway. The sacks were packed full of delicious smelling food.

"How much?" asked Jake, taking the bags from the still smiling boy and putting them down on the kitchen table.

"£35 pounds please mister."

Jake fished out the money from his wallet and handed it to him.

"Thank you mister, enjoy your food" and with that he went back to his moped, turned on the key, ran alongside it for a few yards, jumped on and drove away.

"Food's here" Jake shouted, but Mo and Jess were already there retrieving hot dishes from the oven and taking the bag from the table they began emptying the plastic food containers into them. They carried the steaming food through to the dining room where Jaime already sat expectantly. She'd poured three large glasses of red and a small one for Jake as she explained she knew he wouldn't drink much and drive.

Crispy duck with pancakes, egg fried rice, chilli noodles, prawns in black bean sauce, sweet and sour chicken, spare ribs, spring rolls and beef with mushrooms in an oyster sauce filled the small table and looked and smelled delicious.

"Dig in" invited Mo, and dig in they did until just about everything had disappeared.

"I'm stuffed", Jake said. leaning back in his chair and patting his stomach.

"Not surprised, the amount you ate", Jaime glanced at him side-wards.

"Me, I don't think I've ever seen a woman with such a gargantuan appetite before."

"Don't you two ever stop this verbal sparring?" Jess

laughed, "But then if you did I suppose you'd probably start kissing." Jaime could feel a blush starting to creep up her neck which Jess noticed
"Hit a nerve did I?"
Mo, diffusing the situation, suggested they should get on and discuss the case.
"Good idea" said Jaime, giving Jess a withering look.
"My cue to go and do some marking then" said Jess, rising to leave. "See you later Sis" and as she left she ruffled Jaime's hair.
"Oi" said Jaime, but she was smiling again.

Mo began by recounting the conversation she'd had earlier with the Bishops. Jaime leaned forward, almost perching on the edge of her chair. Jake watched her and having studied body language was acutely aware that she was adopting the classic position of a person who's alert, opinionated and eager to share ideas and feelings -although they may be quite different from his own.
"Any thoughts?" Jake asked when Mo finished and Jaime visibly relaxed.
"Ever hear of introjection?" she asked, looking at each of them in turn. Both shook their heads no in answer.
"Then basically introjection occurs when a subject incorporates the characteristics of another person unconsciously into their psyche. A common pattern occurs when a child introjects aspects of its parents into its own persona. In other words the subject picks up traits from his parents such as gestures words etc. I remember Gus Harrison telling me about a strange case he'd worked over twenty years ago.

Two 14-year-old boys, firm friends, lived in the same street, on the same council estate, did everything together. The dominant one, let's call him boy A, came from a solid working class family background and had a happy childhood. Boy B on the other hand suffered physical abuse at the hands of his alcoholic father. The mother was also abused and afraid so the boy's childhood was an absolute nightmare. In fact, the only time he was happy was when he was with Boy A. In the end he was beaten to death by his father when he tried to intervene and stop a brutal attack against his defenceless mother. Boy A actually saw his friend's battered body lying on the kitchen floor and, distraught, picked up a knife and stabbed the man repeatedly saying "you'll never beat me again you bastard." He then calmly walked into the local Police Station and said I've killed my father gave them the address and waited.

Gus was called in when the police couldn't understand why Boy A was claiming to be the man's son. His own parents were at the Station but he was hugging Boy B's mother and telling her not to worry, everything would be okay now. After spending a considerable amount of time with the boy, his only explanation was that the trauma of seeing his dead friend and, unable to accept it, had taken Boy B's place and was preventing his father from abusing his mother by killing him.

Boy A's plea at the trial was not guilty on the grounds of 'temporary insanity'. Gus Harrison gave evidence on his behalf and the boy was released into his psychiatric care but securely in a private mental health facility. It took time but he did recover and was re-united with his true family.

I have a theory and it's only that" said Jaime, cautiously.

"We're listening", said a fascinated Jake.

"Abandoned, alone in the world and feeling deserted by parents he never even knew, Price considers himself a nobody and suffers from massive self-rejection. Harry, at least, knew why and how he ended up in care and Price above all needed a reason for being there. He stole Harry's photograph, he forced Harry into becoming his blood brother. To him that meant that Berriman blood now flowed through his veins and at that moment in his mind he actually became Harry. He had a new identity and the false memories of a childhood that Harry had shared with him when they were close. What he didn't have, and couldn't adopt, were Harry's thoughts and feelings. Harry forgave his mother, Price resented her - after all she beat him, locked him in the cellar and was the reason he was at Stirling House. A hatred for Isabelle Berriman was born.

Searching for his 'father' and finding him only added to his sense of identity. So when he saw women that physically resembled his "mother" he wanted revenge.

Sound far-fetched?" Jaime asked.

"Sounds feasible to me and it's a possible explanation for the association between Price and Berriman that, until now, we've been unable to fathom." Jake sounded impressed and Mo nodded in agreement.

"So is he insane?" Mo asked.

"Define insanity. Ask six experts and all would probably come up with a different definition. Can Price distinguish fantasy from reality? Probably not, diagnosis insane. Does he know right from wrong? Probably, diagnosis sane."

"Complicated then."

"Minefield, he'd need several weeks of psychiatric assessment to be sure and then it may all hinge on interpretation."

"Do you think Laura Marks could still be in danger?" Jake asked.

"Highly likely. She's escaped punishment so he must be feeling anger and frustration. He's probably desperate to finish the job he started."

"So you think he's still in the area? I thought he might scarper back to Manchester or even leave the country."

"This mother fixation is very strong and his unfulfilled ambitions for her could be a powerful draw. Personally, yes, I think he's still in the area."

"Then it's good that we have a squad car stationed outside Laura's block of flats."

"He gained access before as a Paramedic answering a 999 call and that won't work again for sure. The boyfriend's feeling guilty and always in close attendance. Unlikely he'll leave her alone in the foreseeable future. Tomorrow his E-fit will be all over the newspapers making it difficult for him to hide", said Jake.

"Not that difficult Jake" Mo interrupted, "he's already

changed eye colour so if he changes hair colour and style, grows a beard, he could look very different within a few days. Well different enough to avoid easy recognition, anyway."

"You're right Mo, so how do we go about catching him?"

"Can I make a suggestion?" Jaime asked, tentatively.

"Always open to any suggestions from you" Jake said, with a meaningful wink.

"Get your policeman's hat back on Summers and listen. Would Laura be willing to act as bait to trap him?"

"Not a good idea. This is real life not a plot for one your novels. I can't take that sort of risk with someone's life. She's traumatised enough already." He sounded angry.

"I think if she's willing it's worth a try. We've got to catch him", Mo said, calmly.

"At what cost?" Jake demanded.

"None, if we plan it properly" Mo answered.

"I'll think about it" he said, grudgingly. "Jaime, I'm sorry, I didn't mean to put you down, it was a valid suggestion."

"Apology accepted. I do understand how difficult it would be for you to take on that responsibility."

Jess appeared in the doorway.

"Still working, you've been at it for hours. Anyone want coffee?"

"No, we've just about finished and yes, I'm sure everyone would like coffee", Mo said, smiling at her partner.

"You go through to the sitting room and I'll make the coffee."

"I'll help you love" said Mo.

Jake followed Jaime as she deftly manoeuvred herself into the sitting room and collapsed onto the sofa.

"You're almost running on those things now" he said, taking the crutches from her and laying them down on the floor. "Before you make some smart arsed remark, I rather like Jess's alternative" and with that he bent down and kissed her.

She wasn't expecting it to feel so right, but it did, and she kissed him back. Jake, hearing movement, pulled away and plonked himself down beside her.

"Much better than verbal sparring", he said, smiling.

"Much" she surprisingly agreed.

Coffee arrived and the four of them chatted socially for twenty minutes or so.

"Well, I'm ready for bed", Jess said. "It's Open Day at school tomorrow so I need to be bright eyed and bushy tailed."

"I'm coming too," said Mo, yawning.

"My cue to leave I think" said Jake. "It's been a very productive evening so thank you ladies."

"Don't go Jake, stay and keep me company for a while, I'm not ready to sleep yet. That's okay isn't it Jess?" asked Jaime.

"Of course, just make sure the doors are locked when you leave" Jess replied.

"You're saying that to a policeman Jess. Shame on you" Jake quipped.

"Are you thinking what I'm thinking?" Jess whispered, as the door of their bedroom closed behind them.

"I'm two chapters ahead" laughed Mo.

About an hour later Mo heard his car start up and smiled.

45

Newbury, 1979

Evil comes in many guises, all of them malevolent. None more so than in the shape of 20-year-old Dale Roberts, the product of a brutish alcoholic father and a simple gypsy mother, daughter of a travelling fairground worker. Dale had been conceived in a Walzer car when Jimmy Roberts had unprotected drunken sex with the sixteen-year-old gypsy girl. The Newbury Michaelmas fair had closed for the night and Jimmy sneaked back hoping to get lucky with the daft bitch he'd met earlier. And he had got lucky, nothing memorable just a frantic fuck in a very confined space which turned out to be the most costly mistake of his young life. Marko, the father, came looking for Jimmy when he found out the boy had impregnated his daughter Kizzy. Marko made him an offer he couldn't refuse.
"Marry her or I'll cut your balls off."
Jimmy, being the coward he was, married the wretched girl and they were unhappy ever after.

The boy grew up on one of the council estates in Newbury that flourished in the 1960s. He hardly went to school; his mother never went so why should he be made to. A nightmare at home and in trouble with the police from an early age, his parents were only too pleased that he spent most of his time out of the house roaming the streets with the other two sewer rats he'd befriended.

Frog, aptly named because of his bulging eyes caused by an overactive thyroid, was a skinny mousey haired boy with an acne riddled face. His one saving grace was that he hero worshipped the swaggering, egotistical Dale. Fat TJ was an overweight, whining bully who loved nothing better than to pick on the smaller kids relieving them of their sweets, pocket money and anything else he deemed worthy of stealing. On the estate the trio became known as the 'Untouchables,' not because they reminded anyone of the American law enforcement guys but because they were disliked and avoided at all costs by the decent people in their community.

It was Dale's twentieth birthday and he felt like celebrating. "Let's steal a car and go find us some pussy" he suggested, with a wide salacious grin.
"Yeah man pussy sounds good to me", Fat TJ whooped.
"You up for it Frog?" Dale asked the unfortunate teenager.
"If that's what you want" he said, pointedly "let's do it."
"Here kitty, kitty "called TJ, laughing at his own joke.

An hour later they were driving down the country lanes of Berkshire in a stolen red Austin Metro and high on weed. As they drove through Compton Village the school bus pulled out in front of them.
"School girl alert" yelled Fat TJ "follow that bus."

They followed it to East Ilsley, where it stopped and two boys disembarked, and then through to West Ilsley, where again it stopped and two boys got off.
"Aren't there any girls on this fucking bus?" TJ complained loudly.

At Farnborough the bus stopped, the doors opened and 15-year-old Alice Scott, a slender girl with long dark hair, got off, followed by Jason Edwards, a 12-year-old farmer's

son. After leaving the bus they went their separate ways, Jason walking back in the direction of West Ilsley.
"Hallelujah, at last a girl and a good looking one too. Don't you just love that school uniform?" TJ said excitedly.

Dale hurriedly parked the car and they followed the girl on foot. She turned right into a small road between two houses through to a bridleway and began to walk towards a couple of houses visible in the distance.
"Perfect" Dale said "no-one around let's take her now."

They pulled the terrified girl into a nearby field and raped her again and again. Dale was first, because, after all it was his birthday. Afterwards they just left her lying there in pain and crying.

After a few minutes she struggled to her feet and managed to walk home. She opened the door and started slowly up the stairs. Her mother hearing her shouted from the kitchen.
"Is that you Alice?"
Gathering her strength she answered.
"Yes mum just going to change out of my uniform and do my homework. Be down later."
"Don't you want a drink first?"
"When I come down."
Marie Scott shrugged. Most days Alice came straight to the kitchen and helped herself to a drink from the fridge. Today was different, kids eh she thought.

Alice took off her uniform went to the bathroom and ran a bath. Having scrubbed herself free of those dreadful boys Alice put on her pyjamas and dressing gown and went downstairs. She felt sore and bruised. Seeing her dressed ready for bed her mother raised a quizzical eyebrow.
"Alice?"
"I needed a bath", she said lightly as she gave her mother a hug. "I didn't have time for a shower after hockey practice and I felt grubby. There didn't seem much point in getting

dressed again. I'm not going out anywhere tonight. So that's me ready for bed but not ready to go to bed yet. Can I have a cup of tea mum?"

"Of course you can darling" her mother said, pecking her on the cheek.

She never told her parents about the attack. She couldn't, they were both over fifty, volunteers with the Salvation Army Corps in Newbury and always called her their belated blessing. She wasn't about to destroy their faith in human nature so she kept quiet.

Nine months later PC Ron Price was called to a building site in Wantage where a brickie had discovered a new born baby wrapped in a blanket and dumped in a cardboard box.

A year after the baby was born Dale Roberts was killed when another car he'd stolen crashed into a lorry on the A34 just outside Newbury. Kizzy Roberts, Frog and Fat TJ were the only mourners at his funeral. Jim Roberts was too drunk to attend and, as he so aptly put it, the boy was a waste of space anyway. The pubs were full that night, drinkers quietly celebrating the demise of the devil incarnate.

46

Donnington

Jake woke early, jumped out of bed disturbing Hobbs who was curled up beside him and who complained bitterly at such a rude awakening.

"Get over yourself Hobbs. Nothing, and I mean nothing, will dampen my spirits today."

"Well maybe that" he said as he lifted the blind and saw the dense early morning mist that often blighted autumn days.

"No, not even that' he said, letting the blind fall again and starting to whistle tunelessly, sending Hobbs dashing from the bedroom and out through the cat flap.

"Not very flattering Hobbs" Jake laughed.

An hour later the sun had almost burnt off the early morning mist leaving just a few isolated layers amongst the trees which gave the scene a kind of eerie beauty. As Jake drove the short distance from home to work, all he could think about was Jaime. Not in relation to the case, which should be his priority, but how she'd felt wrapped in his arms. Her welcoming mouth, her lips opening and their tongues mingling as he kissed her. He was embarrassed to find that his thoughts had awakened desire and, with that, sexual arousal. Just as well he was alone in the car.

"Snap out of it Summers you're on your way to work" he

silently chastised himself.

Mo was already at her desk when he walked through to the office.

"Morning Guv" she said loudly, and he stopped and walked back to her desk.

"What did you do to Jaime last night? Drug her? She's usually up and about early but she hadn't moved from her pit when Jess and I left," Mo joked.

"Pleasant dreams keeping her there hopefully" he countered "I think the verbal sparring's well and truly over."

"I'd have put money on that" said Mo, winking and smiling knowingly.

Then her expression changed as she replaced the banter with a serious question. "Think any more about asking Laura to act as our bait?"

"Long and hard" he replied. "I think we should work out a plan, put it to Laura and see how she feels. If she says no, then that's it. There'll be no persuasion; we just drop the idea completely, okay?"

"Okay. Do you want to formulate a plan now?" She asked and, picking up her notebook, started to rise from her seat.

"Give me five minutes to get a caffeine fix, get my brain in gear and then come on in" he said "and, Mo, it's early days yet. I'm not quite ready to become your brother-in-law so don't go buying the hat." He walked away chuckling.

"Oh I think you might be" she muttered under her breath.

Five minutes later it wasn't Mo but Dusty that knocked on his door.

"Archie Jenkins wasn't on duty yesterday Guv, but I caught up with him first thing this morning."

"And?"

"He said that a guy called Harry Berriman fitted the description. A trained Paramedic who'd transferred here from Manchester about three and half years ago. Apparently he only stayed in the job for nine months or so.

He didn't mix much with the other crew members and the guy he was teamed up with a Roy Bellamy, described him as an uncommunicative loner. Said he knew no more about Berriman on the day that he left than on the day he started. Oh, and Berriman had brown eyes and drove a black estate car but not with reflective windows.

"Perfect Dusty, just as we thought, Johnny Price aka Harry Berriman."

"He's told you then" Mo said, as she came into the office.

"Yep it's all falling into place", he smiled. "Thanks Dusty, you and Gregg get over to Chapelgate. Find out how Mike Long and his team are doing."

"Right Guv" he said, leaving the office only to be replaced by a flustered and breathless Halliday.

"Sorry to interrupt Sir, but we have a very angry Harry Berriman in reception demanding to speak to the officer in charge of the Abductor case."

"Wouldn't it have been easier to ring through and tell me" Jake said, rolling his eyes upwards in exasperation.

"Sergeant Underwood was on the phone Sir and I thought you'd want to know immediately."

"Ok Halliday, but you didn't need to run."

"Believe me Sir I did. Mr Berriman is one angry chappie."

"So escape was the safest alternative eh Halliday?" Mo laughed.

"The only alternative Sarge" he replied blushing.

"Right, put the angry man into an interview room and I'll come and talk to him."

"He has a wife with him as well Sir."

"Well take them both there then" Jake said curtly.

"Yes Sir, sorry Sir." The young PC left mumbling

"That was a bit harsh Guv", Mo said, sympathetically.

"Well first it's an angry man and then it's an angry man and his wife. Have they brought the dog I wonder?" Then he laughed "terrified the poor little sod didn't I?"

"Let's put it this way, I don't think he'll be back in a hurry. Do you want me with you for protection when you see the angry man and his wife?"

"Ha bloody ha" and then feigning nervousness "yes please

Sergeant Connolly."

47

Interview Room

Jake and Mo walked into the interview room where Harry Berriman, a man in his sixties with unfashionably long wavy grey hair and deep set blue eyes, looking red faced, in fact almost apoplectic, sat drumming his fingers impatiently on the table in front of him. As Jake walked in he heard the woman sitting beside him say "calm down Harry love, you'll have a heart attack."

"Sound advice Mrs Berriman,", Jake said, as he and Mo sat down opposite. "I'm DCI Summers and this is Sergeant Connolly. I understand you are anxious to speak to me but first let me apologise for the inconvenience caused by the presence of our crime scene officers at Chapelgate. As you can appreciate we have a very serious situation here. You're probably aware that bodies have been discovered buried in the grounds of your property and we, as public servants, have to investigate thoroughly. I'm afraid it will mean a certain amount of disruption for you and your family for a while so that we can complete our investigation."

Mo was impressed by Jake's ability to diffuse what could have been a potentially explosive situation. The apology took the wind out of Berriman's sails.

"Of course we understand perfectly", he muttered "you're only doing your job. It's just that we can't get access to our house, our son or so called son appears to be your prime suspect and frankly I sure as hell don't know what's going on." And then Penny Berriman in a calm, almost detached way spoke.

"Perhaps you can explain DCI Summers."

And Jake did. He spent the next half an hour telling the Berrimans about Stirling House, the Bishops, how the police had contacted their real son and his family in Australia. How Harry had met Johnny Price, the friendship they forged and the subsequent animosity between them. In fact, just about everything except the actual crime details.

After Jake's uninterrupted explanation a dejected Harry responded.

"So we've spent the last three years being hoodwinked by this Johnny Price. We've made him welcome in our home, provided him with renovated living quarters, and now it turns out he's a homicidal maniac using our property as some sort of burial ground. The worst thing of all is that I accepted him so readily, without question. Probably years of guilt on my part."

Penny put her arm round his shoulder.

"I was taken in too, he knew so much about you and your life before I appeared on the scene and now we know how. Hindsight is a wonderful thing. No one could have anticipated this."

"Your wife's right. He does seem a very plausible character. Why would you doubt him?" Mo asked good-naturedly. Berriman just shrugged.

"Anyway, on the positive side you have my real son's contact details? Could we have them?"

"Of course, Sergeant Connolly would you sort that please?" Jake asked.

As she left she heard Jake ask where they were staying.

Five minutes later she returned with an envelope.

"Your son's Email address and I thought you might like a photograph."

Harry tore open the envelope took out the photo of Harry junior and family.

"Well done son", he said proudly.

"That's more like it" said Penny, looking over his shoulder. "He looks just like you did when I first met you."

A grin spread over Harry's face, replacing the scowl and turning him into one happy man.

48

After they left, Mo turned to Jake and gave him a thumbs up sign.

"How to make an angry man happy in one easy lesson. Well done Guv."

"Just one of my many talents Connolly, just watch and learn, watch and learn" he laughed.

"Meanwhile back to business, let's hatch a plan."

Two hours later Mo was driving them to Salter Street.

"You're still not sure about this are you?" she asked glancing side-wards at Jake.

"Not sure, no I'm not bloody sure. I'm shitting bricks about the whole thing. If she goes for it and anything goes wrong, my career's in the toilet. If she doesn't where do we go from here?"

"We're about to find out Guv", said Mo, pulling up outside the flats.

Dan answered the door looking the happiest they'd seen him.

"We'd like a word with Laura."

"Come in", and he ushered them through to the sitting room where Laura sat curled up on the settee.

"I'll make tea", Dan said affably.

Mo noticed the novel Laura was holding 'Darkness and Beyond', nudged Jake and pointed to the book.

"One of Jaime's."

"You know Jaime Mason?" Laura looked up.

"My sister-in-law" Mo said proudly.

"Wow" Laura looked impressed "this is only her second book and I'm already an ardent fan. I can't wait for the next one to be published."

"She's working on it as we speak. I'll get her to sign a copy for you as soon as it's out."

"Thanks I'd appreciate that", Laura said excitedly.

Dan came back carrying a tray laden with tea and biscuits which he set down on the coffee table and then handed out.

"He pampers me" Laura said smiling.

"You deserve it sweetheart" he said, sitting down on the settee beside her.

"Anyway I'm sure you didn't come here to talk about books", Laura said, looking pointedly at Jake.

"No, we come with a proposition and it is just that. We believe that the guy who abducted you …"

"You mean the fruit cake" Laura interrupted.

"Yes him, we believe he may still be here, watching from a distance waiting around to wreak revenge on his fantasy mother, you Laura. While Dan is here I doubt he'll try."

"He'd better not" was the response from a belligerent Dan.

"What we would like is for Dan to move out and you to act as bait. Set a trap to catch him", Jake watched carefully trying to judge Laura's reaction to the suggestion. She remained completely calm.

"Yes he's a real danger to me and to anyone else that resembles his mother."

"Are you saying you'll do it?"

"Not in a million years. I'm going nowhere." Dan answered for her.

"Laura?" Jake prompted.

"Yes I'll do it" she said determinedly. "It will be ok Dan, they'll look after me won't you guys?"

"She won't be alone Dan. Sergeant Connolly, Mo, will move into the building tonight before Laura makes a big deal of evicting you tomorrow."

"So if he's watching he'll see Mo arrive and bang goes your trap."

"That's been addressed. Fortunately Heidi Johnson from flat 43 is of a similar size and build to Mo, and has agreed to help. Mo has provided some of her own clothes and Heidi will leave her flat wearing them when her boyfriend Mitch arrives to pick her up in his car about six tonight. He will go upstairs to her flat and then the two of them will leave together and drive away. About three hours later Mitch will arrive back at the building with Mo dressed in the same clothes and they will enter Heidi's flat, turn on the lights and close the blinds. Mitch will stay in 43 for a couple of hours then drive away. Saturday tomorrow, so Heidi isn't expected to leave for work. About 8:30 am Mo will open the bedroom blinds and walk through into the kitchen where she will be out of sight from anyone watching. About 9am I want you Laura to make a big fuss about evicting Dan. Throw his holdall out of the front window onto the street and you Dan come outside look up and beg her to reconsider. Tell him to get lost and close the window. Dan will then use his mobile to phone Leo and arrange to stay there, pick up his bag and walk off in the direction of Claremont gardens.

Mo will move in with Laura and be ready to react should anything happen. We'll also have men stationed in the back of vans parked across the road and behind the flats."

"Sound like a plan that will work", Laura smiled.

"I'm not happy about this Laura. They're making you a target and no plan is fool proof", Dan said worriedly.

"I'll be fine, as DCI Summers has explained I have a lot of people on hand to protect me."

"Ok let's put this plan into action", Jake said confidently, crossing his fingers behind his back.

In the Park opposite a tall, short haired blonde man with green eyes and stubble on his face walked his dog and watched with interest as the detectives drove away. Johnny Price released the dog from its lead.

"Okay Rover go find your way home, you've served your purpose. Get out of here." He gave the dog a vicious blow with the lead and the animal yelped and ran.

49

Mo arrived home early and explained to Jess that she could be away for a few days and why.

"Just be careful darling and for God's sake stay safe." She gave Mo a big bear hug.

"Everyone's deserting me. You're off on police business and Jaime's staying at a Hotel in Trafalgar Square overnight."

"Why?"

"Her agent came and picked her up for a meeting with her publishers in London and there's some sort of literary function afterwards so she decided to stay over. So I'm home alone tonight."

"You know you'll enjoy the peace and quiet", Mo laughed.

"I know I'll miss you."

"Me too babe, but hopefully I'll be back after the weekend."

Jess didn't voice her fears but she was worried. Mo was putting herself into a very dangerous situation. Her face must have betrayed her thoughts because Mo kissed her cheek.

"I'll be okay, I promise. Let's have something to eat, I need to be back at the station fairly soon."

Mo left the house at 7pm and drove slowly back to

Newbury. She was scared, a lot rested on her shoulders. It had been Jaime's idea to use Laura to trap Price but she had embraced it wholeheartedly. If anything went wrong she would be to blame but Jake would take the fall. Too late, it was all systems go, she just prayed it would work and no one would get hurt.

Jake was having similar thoughts as he sat at his desk. He'd been over the plan several times in his mind. Dan's words had concerned him, 'No plan is fool proof'. He just hoped it was good enough. He looked up as Mo walked into the office.

"I can see by your face that you're worried too."

"Why wouldn't I be, the stakes are high."

"Too high?"

"I hope not."

Mo plonked herself down opposite him and they sat in silence, each contemplating the evening ahead. Finally Jake spoke.

"Heidi's safely installed at Hannah's Health Spa and apparently delighted to be there free of charge. The longer we need to use her flat the happier she'll be. Just one thing I need to tell you."

"What's that?"

"Locks were installed on the entrance doors to the flats this afternoon as a further safety precaution. Heidi has left hers in the zip pocket of your bag so that you can get in. Mitch Reynolds will be here with your clothes about 9:30 pm. You get changed and he'll get you back to Salter Street about 10 pm. Ok?"

"Yeah, ready to roll" she said, unconvincingly.

Just after 10pm Mitch pulled up outside the Salter building. He got out of the car and went round to open the passenger side for Mo. She got out of the car and with the long dark wig and beret in place was a convincing substitute for the occupier of Flat 43.

Hidden across the road the blonde man watched them.

He'd seen workmen putting locks in place earlier in the day. Annoying but he'd find a way round that. As the couple approached the front door the woman removed a key from her bag and on reaching the door fumbled slightly before unlocking it. Safely inside Mo breathed a sigh of relief. Things had gone smoothly so far.

Something was wrong. He closed his eyes playing the scene over and over in his mind. He was observant and something just didn't sit right. He opened his eyes, eureka moment, she'd got the key out and unlocked the door with her right hand but when they went out she'd locked it with her left. Furthermore, when she got into the car she'd opened the door with her left hand so unless this woman was ambidextrous ....! You clever bastard Summers, you've done a swap. You're expecting me to finish off Mommie so you've put Connolly in there to protect her. Now I suppose Danny boy will walk and the trap is set. Well not quite clever enough. Change of plan Jake.

50

Jess had dozed on the settee while watching the late film on Channel Four. Half a glass of red wine stood unfinished on the table beside her. A loud thumping noise woke her with a start. She sat up and realised someone was knocking persistently on the door. Rubbing her eyes she got up and shouted "okay, okay I'm coming."

"Who is it?" she called out as she reached the door.

"DC Miller, Dusty."

"What do you want?"

"Sergeant Connolly sent me."

"Oh God, tell me nothing's happened to Mo?" she shouted as she opened the door.

Jess blinked as she looked at the stranger standing there.

"You're not Miller, I've met him."

"No I'm not" he said pulling a gun and pushing her inside the house.

"What the hell are you doing?"

"Teaching Connolly and Summers a lesson. I know your precious Mo is trying to trap me but I'm having the last laugh. I saw through their subterfuge, not enough attention to detail I'm afraid, so guess what? You get to be their scapegoat."

"I'll scream my head off."

"Not if you want to stay alive. Just sit down quietly otherwise Mo will spend her days dressed in black and mourning her dead partner."

Sure he would kill her unless she co-operated Jess sat down.

"Better." He took out cord from his pocket and tied her hands behind her. "Close your eyes."

She did and then felt the prick as the needle went into her arm. Her eyes flew open.

"What the hell?"

"Goodnight Jess." He untied her, picked her up and carried her out to the car.

51

He saw Mo open the blinds at 43 and waited patiently. He wasn't disappointed, Laura and Danny put on a great performance. It really was worth coming back for. But now it was time to let them know how futile it had been and that he was still holding the trump card.

Jake had just spoken to Mo. She was full of enthusiasm for Laura and Dan's public display of discord. Now the waiting began. Was he watching? Would he make a move on Laura? Only time would tell. He hoped it would be sooner rather than later. The waiting was frustrating and they were acting on a hunch rather than concrete evidence.

Gregg knocked on the door.
"Message delivered to the front desk Guv." He handed Jake a white envelope.
"From?"
"No idea Guv, Sergeant Walsh asked me to bring it up. Presumably delivered by hand, it just appeared on the desk when the Sergeant's back was turned. Your name's printed on the envelope."
"Strange" Jake picked up his paper knife slit open the envelope, unfolded the note and read.

Hi Jake

Hey, I feel I can call you Jake, after all the hunter and the hunted share a certain affinity don't they?

I really enjoyed the scenario enacted at Salter Street earlier. So Dan Williams has left, DS Connolly has moved in and you're expecting me to call. Wrong! Tut, tut, Jake you should pay more attention to detail when you set a trap. I was almost convinced but then left handed when she locked the door and right handed when she came home. Ambidextrous? I don't think so. And then I thought Sgt Connolly could be Mommie's neighbour if she just changed her hair colour and style. Good try Jake, but not quite good enough. By the way, tell Mo that Jess and I are getting acquainted. We're not related, she's attractive so maybe!!!

Perhaps we can trade, something to think about eh Jake?

"You bastard" Jake exclaimed thumping the desk. Price had taken Jess but no mention of Jaime. His imagination ran riot.

"Guv?"

Jake handed the letter to Gregg.

"I've just put my paw prints all over it so you might as well too." Gregg turned pale as he read the note.

"Oh my God, now what do we do?"

"You phone Dan Williams and get him back home then get over to Salter Street and replace Mo. Tell her nothing, just send her back here, and then we'll check out her cottage in Hermitage."

52

Twenty minutes later Mo walked into his office.

"Well here I am. So tell me what's going on. Why have I been called back here without a word of explanation?"

"Sit down Mo" he said gently.

"Now you're really worrying me."

He gave her the letter.

"No, please God no" she cried out, her voice edged with fear.

"We'll find her Mo, I promise you." Jake pulled her up and into his arms.

"The problem is how will we find her - raped, wounded, dead? Can you promise me she'll be alive and unharmed?" She pulled away and looked into his eyes. "No, of course you can't, no one can" she wept uncontrollably and, unable to offer any other comfort, Jake just held her.

A few minutes later she lifted her head.

"Okay panic over, ready for action."

"I think this has become too personal now Mo. I'll take Miller with me to the cottage."

"No you don't Jake, this is personal and I intend to see it through so don't even try to shut me out."

"Okay, okay, I'm just concerned about you."

"Yeah and I'm just concerned about Jess. She must be terrified so the sooner we find her then the happier I'll be."

"He made no mention of Jaime in the note", Jake said hesitantly.

"Why would he? She wasn't there. She stayed in London overnight. Her agent is driving her back this afternoon. Oh God, she'll go mad at me, a police officer and I can't even protect her sister."

Jake, feeling relieved that at least she was safe, visibly relaxed.

"You were worried he might have hurt her?"

"It crossed my mind."

"Pure luck she wasn't there. It was Jess he wanted and Jaime would have been helpless with a broken leg. He could have killed her."

"Not a thought to dwell on Mo. Let's pick up Miller and go find Jess."

Jacko appeared at the door.

"Mike Long's been in touch Guv, they've finished at Chapelgate and he wants you to okay the release of the main house back to the family."

Being instrumental in finding Harry Junior, Jacko had been the natural choice to act as the Berriman's liaison officer. Keeping them informed on a need to know basis.

"No problem with that Jacko. It will be a difficult time for them going back to that house, so close to the cemetery that Price created."

"I'll be on the end of the phone if they need support. They're a really nice couple. Sorry to hear about Jess" he said, looking at Mo with sympathy.

"Thanks Jacko, we're just on our way out to start the search for her."

"Good luck" he said, giving her hug.

They drove in silence to the cottage, each lost in their own thoughts. Miller sat in the back respecting their need for quiet contemplation.

53

Croft Cottage

Pulling up outside Jake turned to Mo.

"You okay with this? Dusty and I will check inside if you want to wait in the car."

"I'm fine Guv, let's just do it."

Mo put her key into the door and found it unlocked.

"She actually opened the door for him. He must have offered a really plausible reason for being here otherwise Jess would never have let him in."

"We know just how credible he can be Mo. Remember how he gained access and kidnapped six women by talking the talk and being believable."

"But to hoodwink Jess", said Mo.

"If he implied something had happened to you she would panic and open up. We both know that and you would too if the roles were reversed."

"Point taken" she said, opening the door and stepping inside.

They went through the rooms one by one, no sign of a struggle. Nothing unusual, even the unfinished wine was a sign of normality.

"She didn't finish her wine" Jake said, pointing to the glass.

"She never does unless I'm here" Mo said, smiling despite

the circumstances. "She always joked that drinking alone was tantamount to alcoholism."

Jake could see that she was close to tears again. He heard a car pull up and putting a finger to his lips signalled for silence. The front door opened and Jaime hobbled in followed by Jackson Fielding, her agent.

"I'm back' she called out and as Jake appeared "I saw the car outside thought it must be you. Jackson let me introduce DCI Jake Summers, Jake this is my agent and good friend Jackson Fielding."

Jake took the offered hand and shook it firmly. Jackson was beanpole tall and thin. His thinning grey hair was cut short and intelligence shone from his bespectacled pale blue eyes. He was dressed immaculately in a light grey worsted suit and looked every inch the successful agent he was.

"So how do you know Jaime, Inspector?"

Before he could answer Mo appeared beside Jake.

"Sorry to interrupt the niceties Jaime but we need to talk."

"God what's happened, you look like shit."

"Reflecting how I feel."

"You're freaking me out Mo; just tell me what's happened."

"Come and sit down Jaime" Jake said kindly, offering his arm and, turning to Jackson "if you would excuse us now, I'm sure Jaime will be in touch."

"Is that okay with you Jaime?" asked Jackson, voicing his concern and feeling dismissed.

"Yes, sorry Jackson but this sounds important. I'll see you soon."

"Okay, if you're sure I'll be on my way", Jackson shrugged.

As the door closed behind him Jaime looked searchingly at Mo.

"So?"

"There's no easy way to say this."

"For God's sake Mo just spit it out."

"Price has taken Jess. He saw through our plan to capture him and he's punished us by taking Jess."

"Here, read the note" Jake said, handing her the envelope. As she read the note her hands began to shake.

"This is my fault" she cried hysterically. "I suggested the trap. Set a trap to catch a rat and who gets caught up in it, my lovely, funny sister Jess."

"No one's to blame Jaime, none of us saw this happening. We know he spends time getting to know his victims, he must also spend time identifying and getting to know the police involved in the investigation. He knows about me, Mo and probably all the others on the team. Undoubtedly he is focused and thorough. He will probably be in touch at some point because, as you read, he mentions a trade. Presumably he means he will be willing to trade Jess for Laura. We all know that can't happen. What we have to do is find Jess before she comes to any harm."

"If he hasn't harmed her already."

"Be positive Jaime, he's mentioned a trade so at this time Jess is most likely alive and well. All we have to do is figure out where he's keeping her. So get your thinking caps on." He put a comforting arm around her shoulders.

"I'm too worried to think at all never mind think straight" Mo said, looking distraught. Jake reached out and pulled her close too.

"I'm hanging on to two very capable women and I need you both to be strong, focus and to help me find her."

They stood there silently for several minutes lost in their own thoughts but gaining comfort from each other. Jaime was the first to speak.

"Okay, I'm ready to stop wallowing in self-pity and get my brain back in gear. Where would he take her? Somewhere he felt safe and was familiar to him. The most logical place would be Chapelgate but that's a crime scene and crawling with police."

"Not any more, the forensic team finished work there late yesterday afternoon and the property is being released back to the Berrimans as we speak. The press and sightseers are long gone."

"Worth a look-see Jake," Mo said hopefully. "He's a clever bastard and Chapelgate is the last place he'd expect us to look."

"Bugger, the Berrimans could be on their way there now. I need to phone Jacko and get him to stop them or we could have a blood bath situation on our hands."

"Thanks for that Jake. Are you deliberately trying to put the fear of God in me?"

"Sorry Jaime, didn't think. I'm used to cops not civilians."

"I'm Jess's sister not a bloody civilian," she complained bitterly to Mo as Jake phoned Jacko.

"Panic over, the Berrimans are at the station. Jacko will keep them away from Chapelgate until he gets the all clear from me. So shall we go and check the place over."

"Yes let's" Jaime replied.

"Sorry you're not invited, police participation only I'm afraid. I think you should stay put as well Mo, it's too much of an emotional roller coaster for you to have to deal with."

"Christ Jake don't patronise me. I may be emotionally involved but I'm police so don't even try and stop me."

"Do we need back up sir?" Miller asked uncomfortably. Aware of the tension, Jake was grateful for the interruption. "Not at this stage Dusty. We don't want to waste man-hours if this turns out to be a fool's errand."

54

Chapelgate

Jaime watched as they drove off, furious at being left behind. In truth she understood why. An untrained civilian could become a real liability; she was a crime writer not a crime fighter.

"Sorry, Guv" said Mo, leaning forward from the back seat "I was out of order back there."
"No need to apologize Mo, we're all worried. Hey, we wouldn't be human otherwise."
"Thanks Guv, so how will we play this?"
"I think we should park away from the property and approach on foot. If he is there he's probably in his own pad, not the main house. We'll check out the house first just in case and then move onto the barn. Okay?"
"Okay", they said in unison.

Miller parked on the main road about fifty yards from the entrance. They walked up to the main gates which were shut. Jake unlatched them as quietly as he could and they moved gingerly across the gravel to the front of the house. The main door was locked as expected so Jake gestured for them to follow him round to the side of the house. The brick built garage, car port and workshop were a later addition to the property and were situated on the right-hand side at right angles to the main house. The gravel driveway separated the two buildings. Both garage doors were closed but parked under the car port was a black Vauxhall estate, invisible unless you were standing in front of it.

"Bingo," whispered Jake, "now we need back-up Dusty. Tell them no noise."

Miller squeezed past the Vauxhall to the back of the car port, took out his mobile and phoned the station.

"We're not just waiting here for back up to arrive are we?" Mo asked, in an urgent whisper.

"We should", he whispered back.

"But we're not" she insisted.

Dusty re-joined them and gave Jake a thumbs' up sign.

"On their way Guv, should be here in 20."

"Good, you stay here out of sight until they arrive. We'll take a look round back."

He beckoned Mo towards the back of the house where another hedge separated the drive from the rear garden. A kissing gate gave access to a patio area behind the house and through it Jake could see the laurel hedge that hid the building they were interested in. Before they went through the gate Jake leaned close to Mo.

"No heroics Mo, make for the gap in the hedge and keep out of sight this side of it. Fortunately for us all the windows are situated on the other sides of the building. I'll try and get a look inside, see if I can pin point his whereabouts."

"Be careful Jake, for you and for Jess."

"If he's true to form she'll be shackled in the basement."

Jake edged his way round to the rear of the building, ducking below the bedroom window he made for the patio doors. Minutes later he re-joined Mo behind the hedge

"He's in the kitchen, looks like he's cooking something, no sign of Jess."

"So you're probably right, she's in the basement. I wonder if it's locked."

"It's not; it hasn't been repaired since we smashed it open. There's just a plank propped up against it to keep it closed."

"What are we waiting for, let's go get Jess."

"The door lock's busted so she's probably shackled to one of the pillars. That means we can't get her out without noise. We know he's armed and I for one don't have a death wish. I know your anxious Mo, but we must be sensible here and wait for back up."

"You wait for back up; I'm going in if only to let her know I'm here."

Seeing the look of grim determination on her face Jake knew it was futile to argue.

"Ok, if she's in there stay with her and keep it quiet until help arrives. If he attempts to come in I'll do my utmost to distract him."

"Thanks Jake" she said, kissing him on the cheek before moving quickly toward the cellar door.

He watched her go silently, praying that Price would stay put until the cavalry arrived.

Shortly after she'd disappeared into the basement the door re-opened and Mo came out with a jubilant smile and Jess in tow.

Jake hugged Jess who was shaking uncontrollably.

"Physical relief causing the shakes", she whispered in his ear. Jake looked at Mo over her shoulder.

"How the hell did you manage to free her?"

"Easy, remember the lab rats had removed the shackles, padlocks etc., so he had no choice but to rope a chair to a pillar and tie Jess to it. I simply cut her free."

"I'll take great delight in telling Mike Long you called him a lab rat", Jake smiled.

"Meanwhile get Jess back to the car, in fact, drive her home. I'll hitch a ride back to the station when this is over."

Dead Ringers

55

They left Jake standing by the hedge and made their way to the front of the house. Miller was leaning against the car when they arrived and, on seeing Jess, his face lit up and he grinned inanely. Mo helped Jess into the passenger seat and then explained the when, how and where to Dusty.

Just as she finished two squad cars pulled in behind them. Inspector Leyland and Sergeant Walsh got out of one and PCs Halliday, Evans, Talbot and DC Gregg out of the other.
"Where's DCI Summers, Sergeant?" Leyland asked Mo. Mo told him and then watched them as they moved *en masse* to join Jake.
"Good luck" she whispered, and climbed into the car, looked lovingly at Jess and drove away from Chapelgate. Hopefully, for the very last time.

Positioning his men around the building, safely away from exits and windows, Jake used the loud hailer to inform Price that he was surrounded, that Jess was safe and that he had little option but to give himself up. It wasn't long before Price, realising it was pointless to resist, came out, hands on head.
"Jake we meet at last. So the hunter gets his quarry", he said, smiling.

"No resistance then Johnny, only brave when women are involved. Sergeant Walsh, cuff him, get him back to the station and get him locked up" Jake barked.

"With pleasure Sir" Walsh answered.

PART 3

56

Daily Post, 10 July 2010

'Coffin Killer' Jonathan Price Gets Life
Jonathan Price, dubbed 'The Coffin Killer,' was sentenced to life imprisonment with a recommendation that he should never be released. Tuesday, after only five hours of deliberation, the jury returned a unanimous guilty verdict against Price on five counts of murder, on one count of abduction with intent to kill and one count of abduction. A hushed 'yes' was heard from victims' relatives in the public gallery. Sentencing Price, Mr. Justice Henry said he had displayed an amoral disregard for human life, killing his victims Jennifer Rawlings, Emma Payne, Sally Fredericks, Donna Clayton and Ellen Hopkins in a most cruel and merciless way. The judge added that but for the timely intervention of the police Laura Marks would, undoubtedly, have suffered a similar fate. Completely calm and showing absolutely no remorse Price looked towards Mr. Justice Henry and mouthed 'undoubtedly'.
Price had pleaded not guilty to all charges, citing diminished responsibility due to mental defect.

The prosecution relied primarily on the testimony of Laura Marks, the rescued victim. She gave a harrowing account of the abduction, being held captive in Price's cellar, the mental and physical abuse she suffered at his hands and finally his plans to bury her alive.

Pathologist Dr Frederick Saunders stated that all the murder victims had died from asphyxia after their supply of oxygen had been withdrawn and the tube which fed it sealed. Dr Saunders further stated that in the absence of oxygen, death would occur between 1 and 2 hours. The bodies were found to be in various stages of decomposition according to the length of time they had been underground. Citing the case of Jennifer Rawlings, Dr Saunders described the scratch marks and dried blood found on the underside of the coffin lid. A positive indication that the victim was, indeed, buried alive.

This information drew gasps of horror from the public gallery as they realised the full extent of the cruelty Price had imposed on his victims.

A loud cry of 'bastard' rang out prompting Judge Henry to call for order and then threating to clear the court.

Physical evidence included the photographic souvenirs taken by Price, photographs of the bodies and the coffins in which they were buried, the basement where Price held his victims' captive, the shackles that restrained them and the pump that supplied oxygen to keep them alive. Experts examining his computer found that Price kept detailed notes on all his victims and on all the police officers involved in the investigation.

The defence case relied mainly on the evidence of two psychiatrists, Dr George Bellamy and Dr James Willmott, both of whom referred to Price's troubled childhood. Brought up in children's homes the boy had no sense of belonging causing frequent bouts of unruly behaviour. He fantasised about his parents and family, eventually in effect stealing the family of the boy Harry Berriman and taking on his identity. Their evidence peppered with medical jargon gave rise to puzzled looks from both judge and jury.

The prosecution countered this evidence by calling psychiatrist, Dr David Lincoln. Lincoln appointed by the prosecution had spent many hours talking to and observing the Accused. He stated that Price was manipulative, definitely showed some signs of mental abnormality, but nevertheless still cognisant of, and responsible for, his actions.

Asked to describe the effect of being buried alive, Dr Lincoln stated in his opinion the victims, totally comprehending their fate trapped in the dark with little or no movement, lying in their own excrement would have panicked and suffered acute psychological trauma.

The Assistant Chief Constable of Thames Valley, Helen Davis, said of the sentence:
'Justice has prevailed, we could not have asked for anything more.'
It is a tribute to all the people who have been involved - not only the police team, led by DCI Summers, but their support teams and all the members of the public who offered information that led to the arrest and conviction of Jonathan Price.'
A picture of the convicted murderer fronted the article.

57

It was early, 7am, but two woman separated by a distance of more than fifty miles were both already reading that report. The first a 67-year-old widow experienced a flicker of recognition as she looked at the picture of Price. It brought back memories of a son she'd once nurtured who had died almost thirty years ago. Killed doing the thing he loved most, 'joy riding'. A single tear ran down her face. Trapped in a loveless marriage she felt only relief when her brutish husband died shortly after. His death was the result of years of alcohol abuse. Her father shouldn't have forced Jimmy to marry her. Maybe then Dale would still be here. Jimmy Roberts had moulded his son's life from the day he was born, turning him into Jimmy mark II.

The picture of the man Price favoured both of them.

Widowed and alone at thirty-seven, Kizzy was not one for self-pity. She enrolled in a literacy class, learned to read and write, got a job, got a life. Two years on and lonely she resolved to find her gypsy family and find them she did. Her brothers Raoul, Jeb and Carlo were all married with children. Her sister Melda was single but betrothed. Her parents were both dead but her siblings were all part of a gypsy community encamped close to the A34 south of Newbury. Re-united with her family and no longer alone,

Kizzy once again embraced gypsy life. Made welcome and loved by her community but shunned by the outside world and regarded by some as a parasite, part of the non-politically correct 'Traveller' trash. Nevertheless she was happier than she'd ever been.

She discarded the newspaper and the memories and made some tea.

The second woman, a 46-year-old wife and mother, saw the face of a rapist staring back at her. A face she'd never forget, belonging to a monster that had forcibly taken her virginity and then encouraged his friends to defile her too. Alice Hawkins gasped in horror as the realisation that Jonathan Price, this cruel calculated killer was his son, no, their son. The son she'd abandoned on a building site all those years ago. He was the image of his father and the name Price was familiar. That was it, she'd read that a PC Price had found the boy. She hadn't thought about him for years and now to be reminded like this was abhorrent. She glanced over to the photograph of her family. Her husband Tom smiling broadly, his arms stretched round the shoulders of their children, Mattie and Joanna. The photograph showed a happy loving family, her family. Her eyes were drawn back to the paper and re-reading the sentence about Price's troubled childhood a tear escaped her eyes too. She was experiencing a 'guilt trip'. Perhaps he would have turned out differently if she'd told her parents about the rape and kept the child. On the other hand his father was a monster so chances were he could have become one too. Would nature have triumphed over nurture? She would never know. She'd kept her secret for thirty years, she wasn't about to reveal it now. No one knew, no one would ever know, this secret would be buried with her.

She'd met her husband Tom at Young Famer's Club in Newbury when she was eighteen and he was twenty. His father was a successful arable farmer in Winterbourne and after he'd died Tom and his brother, Nick, had inherited the farm. Nick, not interested in farming, had sold out to his brother then moved to London to sell antiques and enjoy city life. She glanced at the kitchen clock; Tom would be in for his breakfast soon. Putting the newspaper aside she stood up from the pine table and put the kettle on.

58

Jaime climbed back into the warm bed, her body chilled from her naked dash to the bathroom. Hobbs grumbled at the disturbance, stretched and jumped off the bed heading for the cat flap and the outside world. Seemed he needed a pee too.

Jake was lying on his back, mouth slightly open, snoring gently. She moved closer and nuzzled her nose against his neck. Waking slowly he opened his eyes and smiled. "Stealing again Jaime?"
Puzzled she propped herself up on one elbow and looked at him quizzically.
"Stealing again?"
"Stealing my body heat deserves to be punished, requires a stiff sentence."
"So punish me."
He turned to face her and pulled her into his body. Feeling his hardness pressed against her leg she laughed.
"Ah-ha, now I understand the stiff sentence you're about to impose."

An hour later, sated, she lay in the crook of his arm with her head resting on his chest.
"Not a sentence you thrust upon all your female thieves I hope?" she asked.

"Only the attractive ones."

She punched him playfully before getting serious.

"You must he greatly relieved that the trial is finally over. I know Jess is."

Jaime had supported Jess throughout the trial at the Old Bailey and was well aware of the effect that this trial had had on her sister. After giving evidence, Jess had remained and listened to the rest of the case. Hearing the prosecution detail and realising the full extent of the atrocities committed by Price, Jess realised just how lucky she had been to be rescued unharmed. Not so lucky were the horrified families of the victims, two of which were led away from the public gallery in tears. After Price was sentenced she leaned over and whispered to Jaime.

"I hope the bastard rots in hell."

So unlike her Jess who, up to now and in her own naïve benevolent way, saw only the good in the people around her.

"Relieved yes, jubilant definitely. It's over and we got the outcome we hoped and prayed for", Jake said.

"He is insane, you do know that don't you?"

"Maybe, but sane enough to be plausible, manipulative and capable of planning to abduct and execute his victims. Just deserts I'd say."

"Agreed, I wasn't being contentious, just stating a fact."

"I expect nothing less than full and frank exchanges now I'm living with a psychologist", he smiled down at her.

"Lapsed Psychologist, remember?"

59

7:30am and Croft Cottage was a hive of activity. Mo and Jess were packing. School had broken up and Jess was free for the next five or six weeks. She had things to do to prepare for next term but for the next two weeks it was her time. Newly promoted DI Mo Connolly had taken annual leave, booked a holiday on-line and now they were off to Crete. Dusty Miller had volunteered to drive them to the airport. The flight left Heathrow at 12.45 pm took approximately four hours so, with the time difference of 2 hours, they would be landing in Heraklion about 7pm. Hey, not the best time to arrive but then they had got a deluxe holiday reasonably cheap. Dusty was picking them up about 9:15 am to allow for any holdups, checking in and clearing passport control.

Jess needed this holiday, Christ they both did, thought Mo. Two weeks of sun, sea and sand, total relaxation just what the doctor ordered.

Mo had crammed her case full with just about all of her summer wardrobe and was finding it difficult to close. Jess glanced over saw her struggling and laughed.
"Luggage allowance is restricted to 21 kilos, babe. If you don't want to pay an excess charge you'd better prioritise. Besides you know you won't wear half of it."

"Probably, but deciding which half's the problem."
"Let me look" she said, good-naturedly, pushing Mo to one side.

Ten minutes later the case closed easily.
"There, swimming costumes, shorts, T-shirts and flip flops for day wear and a few nice things for evening wear and underwear of course. Sorted!"
"What would I do without you?"
"Pay for excess baggage." Jess laughed and hugged her.

60

Laura Marks was awake and glad to be alive. The trial was over, thank God. Price was locked up for the rest of his natural and Dan, the new man in her life was lying beside her. He had the same boyish good looks, the same fit, desirable body as the old Dan but this one was totally committed to her and their life together. They were getting married next month. Light streamed into the bedroom, through the flimsy curtains that hung at the window. Yes Dan had even learned to sleep through this daily influx of light.

Coming so dangerously close to losing her life, Laura had vowed to embrace each and every day. She'd even grown close to her mother again after years of being virtually estranged. All teenagers defy their parents and Laura, at fifteen, behaved no differently. Her mother never really forgave her for the bolshie, irreverent behaviour of her teenage years. After Laura's ordeal her mother, realising she'd almost lost her only daughter and that life's too short to be harping on about things that happened in the past, was phoning daily to 'talk'. They met up, hugged, and both apologised for the wasted years.

Dan stirred and sat up wiping the sleep from his eyes.
"Coffee darling?" he asked, kissing her lightly on the cheek.

"I'd prefer nookie darling" she said, pulling him back down.

"No time" he apologised, extricating himself gently from her arms. "You've forgotten haven't you? Your mother will be here at ten, shopping, wedding dress, ring any bells?"

"Not even a quickie then?"

"No, not even a quickie. It's busy, busy, and busy today and then Leo and Sophie are coming to dinner tonight."

"Christ I'd forgotten about that. Need to clean the flat, decide on what to eat" she said, jumping out of bed.

"It's only Leo" Dan laughed.

Leo had been a really good mate to both of them before and during the trial and now, surprise, surprise, he'd actually met someone he really cared about. The delightful Sophie was 5'9" of gorgeous woman. A professional musician, Leo had met her six months ago at a concert in London. Even though he already had some desperate girl clinging to his arm, Leo being Leo still tried to chat her up. Embarrassed for the girl, Sophie gave him the cold shoulder and moved away. Intrigued, he became intent on finding out everything he could about her. Sophie Raymond was a 28-year-old graduate of the Royal College of Music and a violinist with The London Symphony Orchestra. She lived in London in a flat close to the Barbican. Her father was the renowned conductor Sir Charles Raymond and her mother, Vanessa, was a classical pianist. Remarkably Henry Buzzard, God bless him, was a distant cousin and knew the family well. Through him Leo engineered a proper introduction and managed to persuade Sophie that he really wasn't that bad.

Dan was astonished that 'love 'em all' Leo was finally a one woman man. Being loved-up had changed Leo and Laura had actually become quite fond of him and even fonder of Sophie, the woman who had tamed him.

61

Sheep grazed beyond the laurel hedge at Chapelgate. After demolishing the barn and sealing the laurel hedge with new mature plants, Harry had sold the land for a pittance to local farmer Jeremy Gates. As Penny said, the money was irrelevant; the important thing was getting rid of the land and its ghastly legacy. They moved back into their house but neither could settle. Their much loved home had just become a house next to a 'killing field', as Penny described it. So they sold up again and, because of the notoriety attached to the property, lost money on the sale. Unable to decide about buying another house, they had rented a small one in Newbury.

Harry had wasted no time in contacting his real son in Australia and they began to bond again through exchanged Emails and phone calls. About three months after Price's arrest, Harry and Penny flew to Melbourne. Harry and Harry junior, as Penny referred to him, were finally re-united. Spending time with Harry junior, Penny realised that as well as inheriting his father's good looks and, although they had been apart for more than 20-years, he had many of the same mannerisms. She loved his family, Elizabeth and the children were delightful and Harry had only ever been welcoming, no resentment and certainly no hostility in those familiar blue eyes. Yes, the young man had been hurt when his father left but as he explained 'life was too short to bear grudges'.

They didn't dwell on Price and the killings, just told Harry the facts as they knew them. Harry had read reports of the case in the Melbourne Times but until he heard their story he was unaware that Price had stolen his photograph and his identity as such.

"He was always a strange boy, bit of a bully too but this. I can hardly believe he committed such monstrous crimes and in my name", was his only comment.

On their return to England they often discussed what they would do after the trial. It was Penny who suggested that they sell the villa in Portugal move to Australia, in fact Melbourne, permanently so they could be close to his new found family.

Delighted, Harry hugged her.

"You won't regret this. I know how much you liked them and it was reciprocated for sure. I don't deserve you."

"You don't", she said laughing.

They sold the villa in Lagos for a handsome profit which helped to compensate for their loss on Chapelgate.

Being witnesses at the trial, reliving the time spent convinced that Price was Harry's son, was a harrowing experience. But it was over. Justice had been seen to be done and now they were about to embark on a new life in Australia.

62

He could tell by her gentle rhythmic breathing and the occasional body twitch that Jaime was asleep. Jake looked down lovingly at the woman wrapped in his arms. Happy to be there she'd drifted back to sleep. He knew for sure that this was the woman he'd marry and have kids with. He recalled his mother's whispered words to him after meeting Jaime for the first time "make sure you hang on to this one Jake. I'll be so disappointed if you don't" and he smiled.

He'd taken Jaime to that Sunday lunch date to meet his family but warned 'they're a great bunch but Glenda can be a bit overbearing.' His mother warmed to her straightaway and was even more delighted when she learned that Jaime had such an impressive pedigree and was someone who would only enhance the good gene pool she was so anxious to perpetuate. His mother, for all her failings, was a warm-hearted woman who loved her family and he was pleased that Jaime had grown to love her too. She liked Rory and the kids too but had to agree with Jake, Glenda was ok in small doses.

Jake's mind strayed to thoughts of his team and how the dynamics of it had changed. It was much easier to interact socially with Mo now she had been promoted to DI but she still occupied the post of his right hand man at work. Alan Miller had filled the DS post vacated by Mo and was proving to be a real asset to the force. Dave Gregg was still spouting cockney rhyming slang much too everyone's annoyance. Impressed by Halliday during the Price case, Jake had suggested that the young PC should consider joining CID. He was now fully installed as DC Halliday and no longer so intimidated by Jake, his 'Guv'.

Helen Davis desperately wanted to kick Jake upstairs to a Supers job in Reading but he liked Newbury, he liked his team and he wasn't ready at this point in his career to be desk bound. He still wanted to be out there solving crime so he politely declined. Perhaps in a few years' time it would seem more attractive, but not now.

Jaime stirred beside him.
"Why so deep in thought?" she asked sleepily.
"Nothing important really, just thinking it's time we stared making babies and then I thought maybe I should make an honest woman of you first. What do you think?"
"Not important indeed, what do I think - yes and yes" she said, stretching up to kiss him.

EPILOGUE

Daily Post, January 4th 2011

'Coffin Killer' Jonathan Price murdered.

Police were called to HM Prison Townton yesterday after a Prison Officer discovered the dead body of notorious serial killer Jonathan Price. Price, 32, jailed for life for the abduction and murder of five women and the further abduction of two others had suffered multiple stab wounds to the throat and chest. His body was found in a pool of blood on the floor of his cell. 'For Mommie Dearest' was scrawled on the cell wall. A grim reminder of the crimes for which he'd been convicted.

Price was certified dead at 2:15 pm on the 3-1-2011 by prison doctor Patrick Brownley.

It was also revealed yesterday that Price was about to be transferred to Broadmoor Hospital, the high-security psychiatric hospital at Crowthorne in the Borough of Bracknell Forest in Berkshire, England. An 'inside source' inferred that this may have triggered the attack on him.

A police spokesman said that Price had been unlawfully killed by person or persons unknown and that a thorough investigation was now underway to identify the killer or killers and to determine how and why it had happened.

Told of the murder, Ted Baker, the father of Price's fist victim Jennifer Rawlings, said quote 'Whoever did this deserves a medal. I hope they never find out who killed him but if they do I for one would like to shake him by the hand.'

Asked for his thoughts Detective Chief Inspector Jake Summers, who led the inquiry that resulted in the trial and conviction of Price, simply said 'No comment.'

ABOUT THE AUTHOR

Trish Harland was born 70-years ago in the small market town of Huntingdon. Her career as a research scientist brought her to Oxfordshire in 1992 when she relocated to Wantage, where she still lives with her family and two cats. Writing has always been an interest and you can find poems and short stories littered around her home. She has always wanted to write a novel and started her first book, albeit half-heartedly, when she retired in 2005. Trish has finally found the self-motivation to finish her first novel 'Dead Ringers'.

Printed in Great Britain
by Amazon.co.uk, Ltd.,
Marston Gate.